Mary M. B. Yates

Ideals of the Immanent Love

Or the Steps of a Soul from Sunlight to Truth

Mary M. B. Yates

Ideals of the Immanent Love
Or the Steps of a Soul from Sunlight to Truth

ISBN/EAN: 9783744755276

Printed in Europe, USA, Canada, Australia, Japan

Cover: Foto ©Andreas Hilbeck / pixelio.de

More available books at **www.hansebooks.com**

IDEALS ✤ ✤ ✤

OF THE

IMMANENT LOVE:

OR- ―

The Steps of a Soul
From Sunlight to Truth.

LYRICS <u>AND</u> POEMS

BY

HOPE HAYWOOD

[MARY M B. YATES]

Los Angeles:

COMMERCIAL PRINTING HOUSE

M.OCCC.XC.VII

Inscribed
to
My Sisters Everywhere
and
To All Lovers of the Truth.

Dedicated
To the Home.

Preface

MANY of these Poems were published in *The Rural Press* of California, and *The San Diegan,* from 1878 to 1888 under the following signature : they are now offered, with others, in this little volume, trusting they may be welcomed among the many books of the present, by all those who would fain bring this Life of Earth as near to Heaven as mortals may.

They extend over a period of nearly twenty years, and were written out of the fullness of a heart striving to keep alive the cherished ideals of a believing and happy girlhood ; trying to understand the meaning of the bare facts of Life — by robing them in that Ideal which is the real.

They are songs that would sing themselves in spite of Fate, and have often rested my spirit and helped me — sometimes to a sense of Happiness, and to Strength ; and to renewed effort — in "the good fight" always. . . Believing that others will find them helpful and of good cheer, I submit them to the public, praying my friends and critics will read consecutively the poems in the different Books, and so judge each Stone by its every facet. I humbly trust that some, at least, of the inscriptions may be found worthy to be engraved on the foundation of that Building not made with hands.

HOPE HAYWOOD.

Preludes

(Written in Girlhood.)

The Castle of Rock.

(A Picture of the Salt Mines of Poland—500 feet Interior.)

Down, down in dungeons, are furnace fires ;
    Down, far down below ;
Fiercely they glow, those furnace fires,
    Down, far down below ;
Over the hot and flaming heats,
        Is a floor of hard, rough rock ;
And on this floor in deep, dark sheets,
    Waters stand in silent death,
    No ripple stirred by zephyr breath,
        And cover the jagged rock.
But light will show the snowy flint
    Of arching roofs and colonnades,
The floor of waves with rainbow tint,
        Flashing bright in diamond sheen,
        And glancing 'neath the sparkles keen,
    Caught from the colonnades . . . .
    Miners find this hidden beauty
Wrapped in the Castle of Rock.
    The flaming torch reveals the beauty,
Nature—stars beneath the rock ;
And oft they launch their swaying boats
    On the silent, surgeless seas,
And wake the waves as they dip their floats,
        To Life's first eddying tide,
        As on thro' silent caves they glide,
    Across the sleeping seas. . . .
Silver white are distant halls,
    Shining in sudden glare,
And as they near the frescoed walls,
Like gleaming snow in the glare ;

Arches and pillars of marble pure,
 In mighty strength uphold;
Beyond is still the Miner's lure,—
They seek the Crystal Salt—
Within this dazzling vestal vault,
 The mighty chambers hold!

*

Silver hour.

(Written in May, 1868.)

Alone and from home, I muse
 At nightfall's silver hour,
And in its soothing haze I lose
 The weary clouds that lower.

The white ray lamp is burning bright,
 In Heaven's solemn dome,
And wreathes the earth in tempered light
 From God's great radiant throne.

The twilght gleaming gems embossed
 On smooth, ethereal blue,
Display their pointed rays recrossed,
 And glory flames anew.

The wedding hour of day and night
 Is past — and diamond stars
Have sung the holy marriage rite,
 In thought's still music bars.

The glorious lamp — the white-browed queen —
 Rides up the zenith's arch;
An angel trims the sparkling sheen,
 And guides the sapphire march.

The rose has lost Aurora's blush,
    And speaks a sweeter thought;
In night's still, starry, sacred hush
    Her heart with tears is fraught.

The airy, aspen shadows lay
    Mosaic floors of light;
Or chase with gentle glancing play
    The zephyr's luring flight.

Broad shining bands of twinkling rays
    Steal through the branches here;
The quivering lines like magic blaze —
    Afar they dance — then near.

Soft streaming pencils paint the bowers;
    The sun's carnelian dyes
Have faded from the weeping flowers,
    Since day has shut her eyes.

The whip-o-wills resume their chant
    And wake the dreaming night —
Sweet melancholy sounds that haunt
    The woods with sad delight.

Oh, glorious queen, thy holy reign
    Can calm the troubled heart,
When Hope's sweet moon is on the wane,
    This hour bids doubt depart.

A peaceful trust buoys up my soul —
    My Father is in Heaven;
He watches while Time's cycles roll —
    The darkening veil is riven.

A Valentine.

Give me a heart like the lily white,
   Pure as its petals after a shower;
I'll set within a radiant light
   Love's golden flower.
This heart I'd bring to thee, my love,
   Wouldst thou accept the boon.

Give me a heart like the sweet, white rose,
   And Hope be its deep green leaves;
I'll twine forever with life's woes
   The wreath Hope weaves.
This heart I'd bring to thee, my love,
   Wouldst thou accept the boon.

*

Hagar.

The young Egyptian flies at night,
   And wanders in the wild:
She weeps beside a fountain bright,
   Alone, an erring child,

And there the Angel of the Lord
   Shines in her darkened path;
He comes from her remembering God,
   But not to speak in wrath.

Sad Hagar, turn thy steps to home—
   The Angel bade thee go—
Thy Father would not have thee roam,
   Thy tears no longer sow.

The dark-eyed maiden lifts her head—
   Yea, thou shalt reap in joy,
Return again, the Lord hath said,
   No hatred shall destroy.

She lingers but a moment there,
    "Thou, God, seest me,"
She calls the Name that heard her prayer,
    And kneels beneath the tree.

She rises from the dewy ground,
    The streamlet guides her home,
Along the rocky plain, bright wound
    The star-lit wave's white foam.

The lofty pines in silent pride
    Their fragrance breathe around ;
The flowers sleep and softly hide
    On every velvet mound.

And Hagar walks with gentle tread—
    'Tis midnight's holy hour ;
In anger and in fear she fled,
    But now no troubles lower.

Yet, once again, we find her lost—
    And with her dying child ;
In agony her soul is tossed,
    But Pity once more smiled.

"She lifted up her voice and wept,"
    God's Angel called from heaven ;
Her frozen heart had almost slept,
    Despair and Hope had striven.

"Fear not, for I will bless the lad"—
    She saw the sparkling well,
A mother's heart can know how glad,
    And Hagar's step will tell.

And thus when Life's bewildering clouds
    Oft hide our heavenly light,—
That Father lifts aside the clouds,
    And stars the gloom of night.

Book the First

*

A STONE OF JASPER

*

Proem: The Newspaper Poet.

He strikes his harp
Upon the lyre of Time;
Another youth
"To Fortune and to Fame unknown;"
Not that the nations hear entranced,
But "papers" tell his unsung songs,
His airy, fairy castles,
From turret to foundation.
And so — he writes of all his petty aims,
And gilds them with fine gold.

Give place,
Ye fires and salt of earth,
And hear him sing; why not,
He tries with you to tell
The pleasures of the chase
For happiness and truth,
Tho' "Peter Bell" were but the simple song,
And stilted learning — idiot laughter?

For what if Pope did say,
"A little learning is a dangerous thing,
Drink deep or taste not of the Pierian Spring."
The living waters of the fountain, Truth,
Flow free for all the thirsty souls who come;
Let each a diamond grasp.

Shall he not draw from language' lists,
Beautiful words that paint for the soul
Pictures of fancy and feeling?
Shall he not see the summer-day cloud,
With its gold, and silver, and blue,
Its fleeces soft and its filmy veils?
How can he help, if his eyes be true,
And his soul in unison?

Shall he not turn to the shining strand,
Where the shimmering waters lie,
In the noonday beam and diamond gleam
Of light on the wavelets blue,
To the mountains grand that watch the land,
Forever firm and true,
To forest and hill, to valley and dell,
To plains and rivers bright,
To flowers that hide, and the hearts of men,
That throb to Eternity's height?

Shall he not hear the ocean's roar,
Before the tempest come,
And gather pearls and shells of yore,
Still tossed on the breaker's foam?
Within translucent depths,
Seeds and sea mosses lie ;
New garden beds of drifted sand,
Fresh heaped through gates of coral,
The living oyster weeps new pearls —
Precious drops on his briny pillow —
The myriad molluscs live and die,
Their homes in ruined beauty lie,
Unstayed by clinging love ;
But the sea with generous hand,
Throws on earth's golden shores of sand,
New treasures for our glad surprise.

The stars give light to night.
And the sun his gold to them ;
The rain to the waiting earth
Falls with its welcome showers—
While air and earth combine
To bring the summer's hours—
With song of lark, and wild bees' hum—
Those fairies that live in the light of the sun
And drink the nectar of flowers!

Thus Nature's children lend
And interchange their powers,
For the ruby wine of Life,
That lends its glow to them—
And they that glow to ours!

Nature is still the vestal fire,
Where Phœnix spirit lights her torch ;
That sacred altar whence
Isaiah's lips caught fire ;
Where visions touch the heart,
And the depths of the soul are stirred—
Unto the heights of Heaven!

Who shall gainsay these birds of Hope,
With starry wings and songs of faith,
Who sing anew the old and true?
Seeking the new; but the old is true ;
Beneath the wrinkled veil lives Youth—
Beautiful Youth with golden harp,
On which the Angels sang
In the morning hours of Life.

Eternity alone can hear
All the words of Truth ;
Sparks—evolved from flints of thought —
As yearning souls walk over Life's wolds,
Flowery—bleak and barren.

Then let them sing
Their gentle idyls that shall waft along
The heart—as on a breeze of song,
While glancing beams of memory play
Along the spirit's happy way.

Sunlight.

Beautiful glory of Sunlight!
   That falls from a palace above,
To cheer and to guide the spirit
   To an Earthly realm of Love!

Beautiful glowing Sunlight!
   That falls from a throne above—
Gilding our Earth with lustre—
   Like the golden rays of Love!

Teaching our hearts to trust her;—
   Warm, in the Sun's loving ray;
Rousing our souls to faith
   In self, and the newborn day!

Beautiful morning sunlight!
   Waking true hearts and hands—
To work in the strength of Hope,
   Throughout all beaming lands!

*

Sunlights.

Sunlight on the mountain!
   After mist and rain—
Lighting up the summit,
   And the foothill chain.

Soon a purple veil
   Will hide its crown of snow;
Softly sinking from above,
   Through twilight's dusky flow.

Anon, the golden glory
   O'er spreads the springing plain ;
Where grass and flowers hasten,
   At the silver call of rain!

Here the scarlet blossoms
   Vie with green and gold ;
There, the light and riplet
   A sparkling chain enfold.

The pink clouds make the mountains pink!
   My baby poet cries :
" See, mama, see," and turns to bathe
   Her spirit in its dyes.

A soft, enwrapping, carmine glow,
   From sunset's tint of rose,
Flits o'er its stony, rugged cheek—
   And hides its olden woes.

A fleecy cloud of pink—
   That slowly sails—a floating mist—
That rests with love and tears
   Upon the mountain's breast!

Evening Star.

Beautiful evening star,
  Whence comest thy beautiful ray?
I shine by thy light of reflected Light,
  By the light of Love on my way.

O beautiful, holy star,
  With the pure and steady ray,
Thou lightest the soul each night,
  Thou teachest the soul to pray,
With thy steady stream
Of holy beams,
  That come from above,
  Like the truth in Love.

Oh, beautiful, beautiful star,
  With your bright, your tender light,
You touch the heart,
  With a chastened, longing glow,
And lead to the Love you seem to show,
To the rest and peace you seem to know.

No vain rest that waiteth,
  But the rest that doeth ;
For the world, and each loved friend,
Thou shinest—aye, unto the end.

Mist.

What shall we do with these dull, dark days?
    Throw them away?
Or make them bright
    With Love's own light?

These days that seem so long
    With clouds and gloom;
May we do no good
    To make them bloom

With flowers so rare
    That they may share
In the light and youth
    Of To-morrow's truth?

If we but sow the seed
    Today — in the present hour —
To-morrow we may find
    The fruit and flower,

The bliss, the peace, the rest,
    For which we sigh;
This is the only way
    To find To-morrow's day,

To-morrow's sun — the wished-for light
    To make our hearts and homes more bright.
Live for aye in Love's glowing ray,
    And find the right, the only way.

Morning.

Awake, arouse, my soul,
  To another God-sent day;
Awake to the sun of Cheerfulness,
  Live a strong and happy day.

Let Love the keynote be;
  And thou, my song and stay
And then my evening star—
  O, patient Industry!

The secret spring of thoughts,
  Throughout the gladsome day
That rise like sparkling wells
  In the current of Life's way!

*

A Game of Base.

O, the charm of the dimples
As they hide and twinkle
  O'er the boy's cheeks,
Her chin and temples —

O'er the little baby's face,
With a twinkling grace,
  They hide and seek
For a fairy base.

Like fairies' fun,
They play and run
  From temple to chin,
But the cheeks have won!

That dimpling dent,
On grace intent,
    Chases the smiles,
By happiness lent!

That charming thing
Is Beauty's wing;
    As it glances by,
It makes Love sing!

*

The Nestling.

A baby!—a baby! Wonderful life,
Beautiful flower—bud of Life!
Little clasped fingers
Sweetly at rest,
Close to his moving
Scolloped lips!
Little closed eyes
That lift sometimes
To look into mine,—
To him divine:
To look and to listen
To sights and sounds
That waken his soul
To Life betimes:
Sleeping—he smiles,
While the dimples peep,
To show the sweet beauty
The soft cheeks keep;
Wrinkled brows—to know his thoughts;
Wise little owl—downy one,
Who kens Love's thoughts?
Tell me not, he never thinks—
But watch his wee bit soul
Struggle through his eyes' deep blue!

My Rose of Joy.

Topaz and emeralds gleam
And rubies glow,
In the opal flame
Of her changing eyes!

The glancing beam
Of a shining stream
Of merriment, lies
In sparkling, living beauty,
Within her clear and bright brown eyes!

The curls and twirls
Of her twining hair,
Ramble and go
At their own sweet will,
So soft and silky a sheen,
That a sunbeam seems
To have lingered there!

Hear her musical laugh,
That rippling laugh,
While the dimples pass
Like roseleaves cast
On the shining waves of thought,
As she slips her little feet
Thro' the cradle's side,
And laughing tries to touch the floor!

O, Rose of mine! May you drink Life's wine—
The milk of human kindness—and refine
In Happiness, Love and Joy.
May your beauty's gleam
Come from the Soul above,
And bless—after long life's eve
New homes of Joy and Love.

Old Time.

Old Time, how canst thou be
So young and so old?
    My life, it is old
    But my glass doth hold
The Minutes so young—
So young and so bold;
    And I've wrought into gold
    The sands I hold,
With Happiness, sweet and fair;
With her I share
    The Hours I bring
    To the Summer and Spring,
When Nature doth sing
In her heart and home;
    The birds and bees and flowers, all
    Join in the joy that is free for all;
The Sun doth shine,
The Mountains climb,
    And the Rain doth fall;
    While Evening's Star
Doth bless them all,
And fold them in faith
    Till the daylight come—
    Till I bring again the Dayspring's dower,
Till Morning comes, with its glorious power,
And brings again a youthful Hour!

The Meadow Lark.

Hear, oh hear that meadow lark trill ;
Is it not clear and sweet ?
As he whistles so soft, and trills and thrills,
With his happy bursts of song.

His evening song—in the pastures green,
Where he has rested today ;
With his heart full of thanks
For every good,
Since his toil for his food
In the morning's gold today.

His heart but waits for the morn
To come with its strength and power,
To help him to sing, to carol, and bring
New love to the fleeting hours.

More love I'll bring, more love I'll bring,
To Earth with its garden of flowers;
Where a home shall rest in every breast
That findeth my meaning's bowers !

Within, within, is the kingdom of Heaven—
Within your patient heart ;
Bide through the dark, and then the lark
Shall join in your glorious song.

Oh, hear him trill, oh, hear him trill,
His happy, happy song ;
His thrilling, thrilling, thrilling joy,
His glorious thought and song.

His thanks, his trust, his love
For the meadows there
That lie so fair,
And listen to his song.   .

Meadows so rare
In the sun's soft air ;
All specked with the gold
And purple fold
Of little flowers fair.

.

I will build me a nest
Of the brightest and best ;
Why should I not
Gather this gold
That the sunbeams hold,
And the pearly pearl
The soft winds twirl.

He plays on his harp with sunbeams—
His music is so rare—
He sets it where the diamonds fall
From fountains of living springs
That leap in the air,
And the drops that fall
Make music in his ear ;
And he sings, he sings,
He rings, he rings
His joy forth pure and clear;   .
Ah, life is a dower of Love and of Beauty ;
Ah, life is a hope, and joy is a duty!

Hear him! hear him!
Hear that lark—
Like the light
Out of dark ;
Oh, his glorious happiness
Is so sweet, he must confess
The power it brings
To his soul as he sings.
Hear him! hear him!
Hear him sing!

Oh, he makes such music ring,
To my ears and heart,
They almost ache
With the thrilling dart
Of sweetness wrought
From Love's own heart ;
And I could almost sing
His hymn divine.

Oh, bird of the golden breast!
Thou sheddest a ray
Over my way
This summer day ;
And I receive
Thy song and its happiness.

The Sea Shell.

Bright sea shell what dost thou tell
By the changing lights we love so well,
When the shadows pass and the lights unfurl
The rainbows there and the pearly pearl,
The pink and pearl —
When the lights unfurl,
The green and gold,
In the rainbow's fold?
O, beautiful shell!
Thou hast caught and held
Deep in thy cells
All the radiant hopes
That the sea can hold;
All that the sun
Can give to thee —
Thou shinest them back,
So fair and free.
No mortal heart could hold
Such rainbow hopes,
Such radiant gold.
O, heart of truth!
Thou hast wrought in thy youth,
With the sunbeams old
For this fairy gold,
This beaming gold — like joy.
Why dost thou hide thy heart
Under a veil of dark,
Then as we turn,
Show the Love that burns
In thy heart of hearts?

So that thou
Mayst hold thy life
In all its lights,
And hold all life,
That the lights may play,
That the truth may show,
And hope may glow
And the rainbow gleams may shine.
Thro' the cloud that the silver lines,
Beneath the misty veil
There are pearls that shine,
There are thoughts that twine
All life to some happiness.
It is there; it is there with time;
It is there — it is there,
Then seek and find.
With Time and Patience,
Willing and sweet ;
With Hope and the minutes,
Young and fleet;
He brings them — aye —
To those that weep,
To those that work,
That wait and seek.
Happy are we —
Happy ye be —
If ye know these things,
And do them.

*

Eden.

Then banish not thyself from Eden,
Nor let another banish thee ;
Put down the sway of passion,
The hindering doubts and bitter things ;

Determination strong shall win
The right, and conquer wrong.
Begin again the hills to climb, for flowers there ;
In the light of Love's own sunlight glow, and purer air,
Beyond the rocks — they grow more fair.
Tho' oft we lose our way
In dark ravines and valleys
Of black humiliation,
Stay not one moment there,
But let the spirit shake her wings
And fly once more for Eden !
Truth shall be thy guardian guide,
And thou shalt find her by, thy side ;
And fair and bright
As an angel of Light
With wreaths and wings,
And sunbright things;
Find beautiful Earth
A happy clime,
Where Life is divine
With golden gleams
From the Sun of Love,
With pure, clear stars,
But no fiery Mars,
Find beautiful Earth
A spring time glad,
With million hopes and flowers ;
A garden old, with rosy bowers,
Where peace and plenty fill the hours.
O, Love ! Thou kindling power !
With thee, the heart doth flame .
Thou makest every hour
To bloom, and bear
The fruits of Heaven.
Why SHOULD a world
Mean Heaven in vain ?

Bright Morning.

Then shake off the dark,
And rise with the Lark
To the glory of Life and day :
Hear the wonderful chimes
Of Hope's fairy bells,
That ring through the air
As the golden glare
Spreads over the Eastern way.
Hear the Linnet sing
As the white rays bring
A tinge of red to his breast.
See the mountain's hue,
Forever true blue,
In the light of the coming day ;
With dazzling folds,
And fleeces of gold,
It softly, and lightly, and surely holds.

Then up before the sunbeams,
To scan the happy ways ;
Before they are forgot,
And lost in later blaze
That hides the best of beauty—
The early Morning beauty,
Replete with Hope, and Love and Duty.
Listen to the Lark—Listen to the Linnet ;
The Mountain Lark, the Meadow Lark,
That love the sun and sing it!
Ah! sweet, why here? Ah! Life is dear—
This is our only hope—our immortality ;

And now we trill—for Happiness
Is our only hope of bliss ;
We cannot be banished from Eden,
For Earth is our Garden and Heavenly Home ;
While there is Sunshine and Youth—
While there is Effort and Truth ;
While there is Love to forgive —
Love to forgive and forget ;
While there is Patience and Hope,
To cheer the nights long hours,
Earth may have Eden's own beautiful bowers,
With her light and her peace,
Her fruits and her flowers,
Her fountains of youth,
Her springs of truth,
And sparkling streams of joy !

Book the Second

*

A STONE OF SAPPHIRE

*

The Poet's Dream.

I have found a truth — I have found a star ;
    It is a poet's dream — dream of a star ;
A star of youth and beauty,
    A star of love and duty ;
A star of light that shines thro' this night
    And hideth all its gloom ;
It is the star of Hope —
    Of Hope and Song.

I read the truth by the light of a star —
    The star of Hope and Song ;
I read the truth by the light of a star —
    A star that shall do no wrong.
A gleam, a ray, a line of light,
    A glimmer of truth like a star ;
Yea — Heaven's own light shall be more bright
    While my star shines for the Right.

I read the truth by the light of a star —
    The star of Hope and Song ;
I read the truth by the light of a star —
    A star that shall do no wrong.
My mission is here to help,
    To help the world with a song,
To help the earth — with a rosy veil
    I beautify her thorns.

Song of the Stars.

Now stars are stealing forth,
　　Paled by the sunset's glow,
They come like modest worth,
　　But flashing truth must show;
And soon like living beams
　　Those gems and jewels gleam,
And silent anthems flow,
　　While Night sits listening,
Hushed and rapt,
　　By music glad and slow.

Still on that field of blue
　　The stars come trooping thro'
The crystal aisles of Heaven
　　With flashing scimetars;
Their jewelled sword-hilts gleam,
　　Then, silent as a dream,
They stand — with brows serene
　　And glory never dim —
While all the host are voicing
　　Their grand eternal hymn.

They sing of old Earth's youth,
　　Of Nature's holy truth
Since Time began to love
　　Her spirit's varied grace;
They sing, with heavenly face,
　　That Joy's abiding place
Is with the spirit Love,
　　Has hovered o'er the Earth
Since Nature gave her birth,
　　And sung with star and dove.

Yea, Joy shall shout and sing
 With all the sons of God,
When gentleness shall spring
 From every soul and sod,
Yea, Earth shall sing with stars,
 When she shall know no wars,
When Love shall softly fling
 A halo round each brow
And gifts of incense bring,
 Alas, too costly now?

Ah, Love, thine is a costly gleam,
 Thine is a costly glow,
And oft I hear thee chant
 A requiem sad and slow
For Duty lost and cold
 In Pleasure's selfish hold.
Lost — lost — so sad and sweet ;
 Ah, nevermore our souls may meet,
That waiting one we would not greet,
 And we must dwell in lowlier seat.

*

Labor, Hope and Truth.

Labor, Hope and Truth
 Are ways and means to noble ends ;
They are the sunlight beams of youth,
 And with them Life with Heaven blends.

Labor, Hope and Truth ;
 They are the burdens of Life's Song ;
Eternal efforts of true Life,
 That unto each and all belong.

And words of Life are words of Nature
 Spoken to our hearts and eyes;
They are the after-hymns of Truth,
 And daily joineth every creature.

Labor, Hope and Truth
 Find Heaven a fireside
Where happiness and Home
 And swift-winged Love abide.

And oh, how bright this life,
 True life with its aspirations,
With sweet content and progress blent,
 When war no more the nations!

*

War.

O, War! Thou art the grief of nations;
What men in noble stations
Shall now take up the pitying strain
Nor let a world mean Heaven in vain?
For aught we know there is no bliss
For those who make no Heaven of this.

Proud men, if ye are gods,
Will ye be as Lucifer?
And knowing evil, choose ye well,
To choose not Heaven, but Hell?

For War is pain and War is woe;
Are there no arbiters
Between Earth's peaceful million homes,
Than those who bid blood flow?

Oh! Is there naught but sell and gain?
Is it for this the cries of the slain?
Why do ye push men into Hell
When ye might leave them in Heaven as well?

For pain is Hell — of body or soul —
That is what the spirit hath told;
And Earth with her jars is a fiery Mars
With men and fiends to lead its wars.

Our homes shall be the Heaven,
That unto us is given;
The old Earth in the arms of Light,
As seems the rising moon to-night,
While points the evening star — to Right.
Take up and sing the sweet refrain,
That Earth shall yet be Heaven's gain.

With lightsome wing the spirit flies
From flower to tree, from tree to skies;
She skims and soars with birdlike ray
O'er sea and land, then far away
Thro' all the ether's blue gemmed space,
To find that loved familiar place,
Called Heaven, but not one star
Doth seem so dear as Earth — home star!

Then shall we not God's peace restore,
Down hideous War, and sin no more?
Shall man be fiend and not be god?
Doth Eden lie beyond red blood,
The blood of all men's brotherhood?
Forbid it, Shame! Come once more, God,
And place man in the home of Love.
Ah, no! An agent free must choose
Himself a home — to keep or lose.

Eden.

Love's garden old, where man so bold,
Has left us out, since Eve once told
This truth — that for Adam's sake,
She dared do wrong — tho' her heart must break
And her home be lost in Eden!

But men shall awake
To this truth for Love's sake,
That home and peace are Eden;
Not Eden alone for a selfish soul,
But for Earth — and all her heathen!

Error.

Ah, Right should have the strength of Might,
And with a heart as hard as steel—
As soft as Love—yet, true as steel,
Be able to stand firm,
Nor ever waver at the dart
Dealt by some careless, faithless heart
That strikes to ruin Hope and Heaven
At one fell blow; at one dread blow,
Would thrust the Right
Back to a greater woe.

Ah, Love! Thou sacred power,
May we know thy truth,
And feel thy strength
In this trying hour.

I will *not* doubt man's truth,
I will not doubt his arm,
I will not doubt his strength
To right the wrong,
To save from harm;

But now we must watch all the ways
Thro' all the blaze
Of fiery trials,
And lift up Love's truth,
Tho' it lie in the dust.

*

"There Shall Be No More War."

Fair Earth shall be the haven, Eden,
Where winds and waves at starry even'
Sigh and rest, and twilight brings
The voice of song and softly flings
The light of Heaven's brightest star
On ways of Peace and balmy quiet,
A garden old where poets walk—
Oft walk with God, and learn
That Earth means Heaven,   .
Would men but find
Sweet Peace and rest,
Would men but choose
Sweet Peace and Eden.

Joy! Joy! Ring the bells!
For Earth shall be free!
Sing, sing ye wells,
And mountains with me!
O, might I express,
In its truthfulness,
The bliss and the rest of the free!
Free from the pain
Of a hope—not in vain,
Since Peace shall be found
On the Earth once again!
Yea, Peace shall be Earth's,
And Heaven her gain!

Book the Third

*

A STONE OF CHALCEDONY.

*

Dumb.

Oh, God! how canst Thou let Thy creatures be
For man—in pain, in helpless agony?
Surely, for them there is no God
But fiendish power—and man, their God!

Wounded and dumb—
Poor suffering one!
'Tis Torture's hour.
O, evil power!
Sweet Pity drops
Her faltering tears
Upon thy lot—
Upon a grave of happiness!

Thy spirit is broken;
Oh, give some token
Thou'lt conquer the spell
So fatal, so fell:
Thou hast a sorrow
That knoweth no morrow;
Oh, *will* the power
To spring from the grave!
Oh, *will* the power
To wait; be brave.
Oh, find some hope
That yet is left
For thy poor heart lost
In this wilderness
Of pain and woe;
This depth of pain,
This depth of woe!

Thou yet may'st know
Some other hour,
Some waiting joy,
Some glorious power;
Some heart caress,
Life's tenderness;
Some love-note pure
That shall endure;
It waiteth long
But it waiteth—aye,
For the hurt and the wrong!

Ah, *can* ye know
Our wretched power
For pain and woe?
Our helplessness?

Ah! Nature, bless
This poor heart's bitter,
Deep distress;
Time, with thy loving hand,
To lift this wretched doom—
Fly fast, come soon!

Fling care to the wing!
Tomorrow may bring
For this bitter pain
Some sweet alloy,
Some gentle joy;
Life *may* be Sorrow—
But Life *may* be Joy!
Life may bring Death,
But Death may bring Joy!

Ah, ye who can,
The brave and strong,
Still lend a hand—
To Happiness;

The Earth hath need,
And dumb souls bleed.
Lend, lend thy hand
To Happiness,
Thy faithful arm to helplessness;
Remove *some* pain,
Some bitterness;
The Earth hath need,
And dumb souls bleed.

*

The Cry of The Heart.

Love we our God? Nor day, nor night
Can hide from men the hilltop light;
Our pain shall be the strength of God,
Our love shall be the truth of God.

Oh, that pleading human cry,
Pleading for a Father's love;
Does He hear Earth's children cry,
The helpless ones? What bitter pain
To see a cripple's wretched chain —
An idiot's pall — thrown instantly
Over a blind heart's beating love,
Because *He* lets it fall!
He held not back the hand of Fate!
Ah, Tell me; Is *this* my Father's Love?
If I but knew I could submit.

Yet, should we lean in fear of harm,
On God's *right human arm*,
Not all the yearning Earth could save
From Death's lone sea nor trouble's wave.
Held fast, why do we struggle
Within the toils of Fate or God's more stern command?

Deep is Death's river and dark,
Dreadful and dark the ocean of Doubt—
We are storm-tossed, but calm is our sleep
After the waters are crossed.
Cease, cease, vain soul, for *Grief must pray.*

Thou knowest! Yea, *our God,*
Doth our affliction know!
And oh, poor lonely heart,
'Tis blessed faith can say—
No other God is like to thine,
No finely spun philosophy:
Thy Comforter! The conscious God,
That knoweth all the way!
Hold fast thy faith,
Thine anchor need not move,
Earth cannot prove
Thy Guardian *is not* thine;
Yea, Christ affliction's way did know,
And *Holy Spirit, Thou dost know!*

✳

Alpha and Omega.

Oh, God! that we might trust!
That we might *rest* in Thee.
Then *must we trust*
In Nature, as in Thee!
Nature, Almighty Power,
That doth create and bless
Her Universe,
Is the Eternal Alpha!
To her flowers she dowers
An instinct for her light,
While to each soul she says—
I also am the great "I Am;"

God is the thought,
My presence lends to thee;
God's Spirit is the love of good;—
Choose ye, my children, always, Good.
Rest! rest on Nature's breast,
Upon the holy arm of Love,
The patient strength of Duty:
This is the God I've taught ye,
Taught ye this glorious Beauty,
And gave ye mind and heart
To help me in my work;
To do your part
To bless mankind;
To be the sons of Good—
The brothers of a Christ;
Loving the poor and lowly,
Helping the weak;
Rejoicing and giving sympathy;
Praising my lilies,
Blessing all little ones,
And in every Garden of Gethsemane,
Drinking the bitter cup,
I send thee—
Till the Day dawn;
Finding the Peace of Christ
To stead thee; that spiritual peace
Gvien to those who seek;
In the nature of things,
In the knowledge of things—it lieth,
Nature and God are One upou the heights;
Nature is—that Infinite Intelligence
Thou canst not comprehend;
Is she not worthy to be feared and loved?
Fear her judgments—love her grace—
She hath apportioned *all* a place;
She lends herself to Man.

She crowns him as her glory;
Yea, Christ is her Omega,
Her highest, best and last.
She hath lent unto her children—
Canst thou not thus lend
Unto thy brother's keeping
What *thou* may'st shortly gather
Before Death's fiat call thee?
Rest! rest thee and submit
To the inevitable.

*

Life.

And if this world were all,
Yet would I willing sooner sleep
Beneath Death's awful curtain deep,
And bid farewell to Life,
With all its sweet redeeming promises?
To Nature's kindly face,
That has so often smiled?
That real and loving Presence,
That doth encircle worlds and men?
Oblivion? I would not say farewell
Until I must; I love thee, Life,
As God, Himself; and it is Nature's will,
That men should love her; love sweet Life
And live, aspiring to some noble end,
Enduring all that Fate shall send.
Find heavenly Mercy's world-wide work to do,
Refine and purify; evolve the true,
And patient, wait as Nature waits,
Upon her own true force and plan.

Live! Live for Earth's future!
Let thine influence be
An onward ray of light
That shall shed light on other souls;
A golden star,
That circles to its utmost verge
To help and save.
There shall be many saviours,
Many stars to light dark souls,
For Christ loved not himself,
But all the world.
Wouldst thou not then
Thus glorify Omega.

For Nature will no more;
 She only gives thee sweetest Life
And Time; thy friends,
Thy children, Duty, and
The knowledge of her face.
Then prize them while they last;
Prize Life and Love
With all their sweet and great rewards!

∗

Mortal and Immortal.

Our darling babes are not immortal then?
Nor Nature's flowers; but yet
She spares not them to love and bless
Her life, her home, her hours;
Life takes our babes for flowers
As fair as those in Eden's bowers,
And keeps their happiness as sweet perfume,
Both when they're here and when they're gone!

Not knowingly, perchance you say,
Hath Nature wrought her gods of clay;
Atomic force, you recognize,
In all her handiwork, and man,
Her highest form of Thought;
How know you that the questioning soul replies;
How know you who may think beyond the skies?
Attraction is a law and Thought,
Imponderable force;
Since Nature has thus formed this world and things,
If other worlds beyond have life that sings,
According to Love's high behest,
Perhaps we have some other tryst,
Where subtle Thought and souls may meet,
And something else of Nature greet.
When we have crossed Death's midnight sea,
Our loved and lost at home may be
'Mong other lives—allowed to learn
How immanent the Love that burns!
There we may learn new ways of God,
And find new meanings for Earth's sod;
For there we know, in God's far sight,
Suns still divide the Dark from Light:
Unknown to us, yet with dear Life's sweet grace,
May fly—thro' God's far-reaching space,
Where other worlds in radiance swing—
His Angel types, who teach and sing,
Intent on Love's work, as it rolls,
Upholding stars and helping souls!

Clearer Vision.

And those we mourned when Death had called them,
How sweet to think
They sometimes come and give a thought to us!
That while we grow to clearer vision—
And toil along the years,
And farther up the way—
They sometimes come and turn our thoughts,
And thereby set us tasks
That we think self-imposed!
They, with their clearer vision
From heights supernal, in immortal airs,
Would fain help still the human race,
Their olden friends and kindred!
We carry on the good work still,
We love the the joy of helping, saving,
But, oh! sometimes I'm fain
To thank the ones who've gone before,
And wonder if they do not help us, more
And better than we know!

Book the Fourth.

✳

A STONE OF EMERALD.

✳

After the Rains.

Shine out, sweet Sun, once more,
And come again to Earth
With thy exalted Love,
That doth our strength renew:
Dispel the mists of doubt,
Of darkness and of fear.
When the sun shineth the earth is so bright,
Keep us in hope thro' hours of night;
O Light, bright Light,
Come to us after the long, dark night.

Far—over the sun-bright hills—
He bringeth the morning bright;
The mists that rise
From the Earth to the skies,
Are grateful prayers to Heaven;
And Earth, with her hills,
And rocks, and rills,
Joins in the joy of love;
While softly and safely, the cattle and birds
Sing the sweet hymn they have found:
"Love, beyond the orient meadows,
Floats the golden fringe of day."

O glorious Day! Thou art true life,
With liberty and movement rife;
Eternal life that lives and moves—
The very breath of God who loves!
Beneath thy smile the Darkness flies,
The shadows flee and voices rise
To praise thy fair eternal skies;
Beneath thy quickening ray
New seeds spring forth; fresh flowers unfold,
In secret deep retort is wrought new shining gold,
New gems are found; new germs expand;

New songs resound; o'er all the land
Bright birds and insects fly
And every heart doth sing,
Beneath the brilliant flash
Of glorious morning's wing!
Thou art beauty, and truth and joy,
Thou shinest more and more—
Unto the perfect Day!

✳

Sungold.

The morning star grows dim—
And silver streaks of light
Shoot over the horizon's brim;
The mountains stand with veils in hand
To veil their frowning brows—
When the sun's glory dazzles them;
He shines forth—now—
With banners that fling
A radiance there—
O'er beauty and blue
In Earth and Air!
With mantle of gold,
And broidered fold,
Of rose and pearl;
With fairest blue—
And shimmering, filmy
Gold of Light—
That streameth through,
And blesseth sight!

And under the tender, smiling skies,
Far off in tranquil distance, lies
The calm, the deep, the beautiful blue,
That mirrors the pearly fields of air,
And woos the tints of beauty there!

A strip of sand—a bar of gold;
A silvery cliff with castle old;
A purple headland, tall and bold;
Broad tableland, with flowery wold—
With emerald fields and shining shields
Of shells and sand—these hide the land
From barrenness—with magic wand.

*

Sunset

O, mystic pictures true:
Of rose and gold
With purple fold,
Royal and rare;
Flung on a canvas of blue,
And hung in the radiant air,
In a gallery free
That joineth Earth's gardens fair!
'Tis only cloud gold, after all,
It will not last; but yet,
The Sun—the Sun himself hath wro't
Those hues we fain would keep;
And long as time shall last
He will renew the golden cloud—
The rosy veil—as Love itself will do;
As golden Love alone can see,
Life's rosy, golden hue.

*

A Vision.

Her drifting hair—blue ether air;
And on her temples fair—
A crown of stars like brilliants set;
Ah! lovely Night is there!

Music of Skies.

Oh, the beautiful, beautiful music of skies
The glow and the glisten of Heaven's own eyes,
The gold and the blue, oh, exquisite hue!
The rosy flush, the purple and dusk,
Night's mantle of twilight, and quiet and hush,
After the battle, the roar and the rush.

Now cometh afar—Night, with sweet silence,
And soft beaming star; with slow dropping dew,
With rest and the fragrance of roses and rue;
Sleepy-eyed flow'rets and glimmer of gems,
Sparkling in starlight on dark beaded stems:
With shimmering radiance of luminous stars
That float in the far, floating blue,
With glory of gold and glory of silver hue,
With crown of points and halo of light,
Each reigneth o'er an hour of night.

O, faithful, shining stars!
Ye sing the angel song;
'Tis God's light on your brows;
Ye are the angel throng,
Keeping your watch till now.

*

A Nest.

I hear a morning song;
In a shadowy bush
Sings a joyous thrush,
    As if to sing—
That sweet content
    Is aye the spring
    Of Joy's own joyful ring!

Nought but a nest—
But the care—sweet zest,
Brings joyance and rest;
    So thrilling, filling
Fields with song,
    He works content, and lives
    His blessed bird-life long.

*

The Egg.

Beautiful cell,
With freshened gleam,
And pearly bloom
    On thy oval shell—
    What dost thou tell?
What if the egg-cup will not hold
Aught but its own, its unwrought gold?
    It yet may be
    The germ of a life-hope,
        Full and free;
A life that shall fill
    A world full of nestlings
At its pure, sweet will,
    When its own unfolded growth in time
    Shall have run its course to an end divine:
Shall shelter them there with folded wings,
And its sweetest song be the one it sings
    To the brooded love of its daily care,
    That it shelters and loves, tho' the world is fair.
Say, what would we have thee be—
But an egg—to all eternity?
    What would we have the egg-shell hold
    But its own full heart, and its own true gold?

Satisfied: A Morning Rapture:

O, longing soul, what is it stirs?
Why beat thy wings continually
Against thy prison bars? Canst thou not sing
Within this mortal frame enough?
Art thou not satisfied to dwell
Within the temple Nature wrought,
To wear the vestment she decreed,
While nobler praise she sought?
Thoughts are thine angel wings,
Mortality thy soul's expression.
Yea, sometimes, shalt thou soar
Unto God's starry heights, into infinitude;
But work-a-day within this working world,
Is thy near gift; body and field for use.
Then, wake! Each morning, with God's likeness
Thou shalt "be satisfied;" thy soul shall sing,
And thro' the Earth and universe,
Shall "Heaven and Nature sing!"
The Dayspring's constancy and glory show His face,
His work with song fills every sphere and space;
When life with duty's beauty is so filled,
Thy heart with love and upright strength so willed,
Thou too shall sing that paean's constant note,
And o'er the busy world, thy joyous echoes float.

*

Word Music.

Sweet cadenced rhymes, whose lingering chimes
Still haunt the soul with Melody's soft spell;
With Music's fond and flowing wave,
And silv'ry rolling swell!

On the Seashore.

The birds by the sea, the swash of the waves,
The dip of swift wings, the waterswept caves;
White sand and bright shells, the red-feathered moss,
The purple seaweed, its soft, silken floss;
Blue water and sky, and glittering shine
On the wind-waving waves of the far-reaching brine;
To each heart comes a feeling that is born of the ocean,
Here only awakens this strange, deep emotion—
A rapturous peace, 'neath his thunder and motion!
We wander by shores where the years are as days;
Rockbound, they awaited the Ancient of Days,
And met the red glory of first morning rays;
Then to the rockribs came the slow-moving sands,
And sinuous shells with the tide to the lands,
Where now we may wander with treasure-filled hands.
With the beat of the waves our hearts keep the time,
Swift rises to rhythm the answering rhyme,
And raptures with ocean and melody chime;
Sweet stirrings of rapture, 'mid sunshine and song,
When morning with dewdrops and fresh flower throngs,
Calls forth the sweet love that to fair Earth belongs;
When breezes and birds, and far dashing spray,
The roll of the waves on the golden beachway,
The silvery crests of the curved bending swell,
So often and often the old story tell:
To the cliffs and the rocks with their towering fronts,
They utter caresses which sound in their chants;
How they ever shall cling to their time-loved haunts,
And dwell with sweet faith by their baptismal fonts!

Sailing.

Come sail with me
On the silvery sea,
While wavelets sway
And lightly dance,
When moon-beams glance,
And swift winds softly play.

On o'er the deep
And darkling sea—
Her gleaming fields
Shine o'er the lea.

Music doth ring
And our spirits wing
With glories that fling
Their radiance bright
O'er the sea all night;
We flow thro' the waves
To the light stilly caves below.

Slow gliding we go
Where anemones grow,
Gray, purple and pink,
'Mid mosses they shrink,
In gardens and groves,
On white rocks where droves
Of parrot fish feed
And hide in sea-weed.

In the mermaid's bright cave,
Where the silver-lit wave
Shines with the curving blue lance
That Luna drops down
From her white-crested crown
On the water's soft sheeny dance.

We have anchored our bark
By her shell strewn ark,
And enter her covert fair;
Here nodding we rest
While fancy's oar breasts
The sea and the storms of care.

But the mermaid's voice rings,
While the lost sailor sings,
No mortal shall dare
Abide where we are;
The seas be our throne,
Other worlds be your own.
Swift these spirits shall hie
To the fields that lie
Round earth and air
And twinkling star.

Up thro' the glassy green
Our gliding sail is seen;
Again our eyes behold
Fair morning's star of gold.

*

The Gate of The Day.

Thro' the beautiful gate of the day,
    My soul is mounting high,
    Like a lark, to the gold, blue sky—
O'er the Earth on her Heavenly way.

The beautiful gate of the day;
    Morning! with golden light,—
    Joy from a holy height,
Flooding my lowly way.

Stay! Till the noontide day,
   With its burden and burning heat,
   Shall a worthy workman greet,
With a meed of rest by the way.

Rest, that is gained with the day,
   True, as the action and soul,
   Sure, as God keepeth the whole
World that is taught on its way.

Won, like a star from the day,
   Worn, as the evening's crown,
   When the swift flying day is done,
   When the beautiful gate is down,
And the heart recounts the way.

✳

Singing.

He sings at night
Like a star of light!
Sweet mocking bird —
I heard, I heard
Thy silvery song,
Thro' the night so long.

What is thy joy,
And faith so bright?
Is there no alloy
In the moon's white light,
As it streams o'er the hill
With its flood so still?

While murmurs the sea,
Afar o'er the lea,
When the shining waves
Sweep shore and caves,
And the tide sets in,
With the windharp's din?

While flowers fill
Their cups at will,
And star eyes glance
When breezes dance,
And rocking sway
Thy nestvine's spray?

But the shadows creep
Where the white rays peep;
And the misty cloud
Makes fear seem loud;
And the death-watch ticks
'Mid the darkness thick.

The wild rose pales,
And the cuckoo wails;
Afar in the dingle
Where wild weeds tangle,
And nighthawks keep
Their circling sweep.

But bravely and bold,
His song ripples out
O'er the shadowy wold;
With never a doubt
In his trusting breast,
He sings he is blest!

For a world so fair,
For his nestlings there,
From day unto night,
From dark unto light,
Sweet thanks must share
His daily care.

June.

Spangles of dew drops, sprays of roses,
Tangles of briars, and snatches of song!
Far down in a greenwood lane,
The wild briar springs, and flings
Its arching sprays and rays,
        Of rose vines red;
They shine and glimmer there,
With dewy pearls and leafy curls,
Swinging in clusters where
The summer's gold is seen,
Thro' whorls and twirls of green.
Near by a mockbird sings;
In a meadow fair,
With royal tints
Of purple rare
And deep sea green;—
While twinkling stars,
With yellow rays
And disks of darkest blue,
Gleam all the grass waves thro'!

✳

Roses—A Christmas Idyl.

Oh, Roses! Sweet roses! Oh, wild and tame, so fair!
Since when ye left bright Eden, the fairest flower here;
Your velvet, pink, clear petals, your shining notched leaves,
Your subtle, balmy fragrance that wind and sun enwreathes;
With all sweet, youthful hopes, and every blessed joy,
Thy beauteous life is bound, may nought my rose destroy.
From tiniest rosy gleam, all veiled in tender green,
To full and faded sweet, unheeded and unseen,

Oh, pale and pure! When white, with waxen leaves,
All wet with early dews, ye come to bind the sheaves:
When round the precious dead, ye twine your clasping
       hands.
And say 'tis harvest home; the wheat is now in bands;
Good seed for other years is like thy faithful spring,
And like the Rose of Sharon, and lilies Christ did bring;
Returns with certain sun, to bloom and bless and wing,
Where God's new song is sung; where Love's redeemed
       aye sing.

*

El Monte.

Rest a while in this woodland dell,
Where the music songs of wild birds swell,
From far off glens and mountain nooks
  Through deep green aisles of dark live oaks,
Here are filmy ferns of lace,
And nodding plumes of Maidenhair,
Hid in the many clefts of rocks,
With Silverleaf, and Goldback,
And downy Clevelander!

Now up the inviting hills,
With lightsome step and true,
Over the rocks—we've sped in thought—
On and up to the very tops,
To rest and see the view!

But the way is long and steep,
And oft we must renew
Our fainting courage, with the cheer
Of little friendly flowers,
That smile along the way,
And beckon to our hands

And ferns and flowers, whose names
We need not tell; they dwell in sweet content,
Oblivious to praise, save when you thank them
Because the world is fair!
Ah! Nature is their own dear mother,
Who gives their dainty robes and bright, clear faces
To seek the light of Day, 'mid wild bees humming,
And happy wild birds singing—
To Nature's sun and glory!
This only is their duty,
To blossom by the way,
And lend to Nature's life
The tender rays of Beauty!

Ah, me! That ruthless Art
Should ever touch this lovely little park,
So dense, so cool, so dark,
So dear to Nature's heart—
Since planted by her mother hand
To beautify her creatures' land!

Mimosa.

O, sensitive flower!—sweet wayside dower,
I loved thee well in thy ferny dell;
Thy purple pink, round ball of gold,
Hath heart of grace in its tender hold,
And doth enfold Eternal things;
'Tis Love divine thy rays enshrine,
For thro' thy glorious beauty shines—
The kindliness God's thought doth hold,
By the side of the ancient rock
In the green and mossy velvet mold,
Thou springest bold;

But thy quivering leaf—a fear must hold,   •
So sure it seems to feel
The stranger's presence there,
In its own soft, balmy air
Where it stands so peerless!
There, where silv'ry lichens cling
To the mighty rock,
Beside the mountain spring;
Where wild rose tangles
With twelve o'clock, and lady slipper:
Royal blue, with golden hue,—
Saffron, and ruby spot!
O wildwood flowers, I loved you well,—
Then will you not your secret tell?

Why do we bloom? We live to bless
Earth with our own sweet happiness!
To wake the infant heart—the grateful soul,
To wonder and to praise;
To love and bless
The Name of Nature!

✳

A Spring Day.

In the sunlight!
The words are a poem,
The thought is a rythm;
In the morning bright,
In the early light,
When the world is fresh and fair!
O, morning fair! O, golden air!
My heart is stirred like that mocking bird's.
He joyously sings—his sweet music rings—
And to the wide world another song brings.
But still, the same sweet old conceit!

Beneath the cloud swept sky,
Slow, silv'ry masses moving by,
Fair hills and vales
Lie half in shadow,
Half in light,
While mountains round
And far beyond,
Engirt the fair, vast plain,
And look unto the sea.

Now thro' the soft, still air,
And thro' the golden light,
There comes a restless thrill;
The wind awakened trees
Stir all their shining leaves;
Now wave the happy trees
Their lustrous lace of leaves;
Now nod and sway
To whispering breeze,
All emerald seas,
And rustling spears of hay.
Now dance and play
The leaf-wreathed stems
On every mound,
Some flower-encrowned,
And wrought with gems;
Some hiding gay
A wee, wild deer,
That bounds away
Like lightsome fay.

Our footsteps rove
To cull the flowers Fancy loves;
Painted cups—a banded bee
Sits here and sups;
Flowers' eyes, like fair blue skies;

Earth's flower stars and rays,
That shine along her lowly ways,
Some speak in words almost, and some
In silv'ry silence, spell the air
With golden thought, yet scarce more fair!
Here, crinkled leaves and tendriled curls
And some are fringed and beaded,
With shining, glistening pearls,
All striving, growing, blessing,
They make my heart strings swell,
And rapture's thrill—
Like Nature's answering own:
Her children answer to her cry,
Thro' all the Earth unto the sky,
When winds and waves,
And rains and light,
Come quickly at her call,
And bear her love to all.
Then they begin
Sweet striving for her blessing,
Or is it only thus I'm guessing?

✳

The Golden Ships.

Now overhead the wide fleet spreads.
While soft and deep
The bright blue sweeps
Around, above each field and grove.

Engilt with gold;
Embossed with bands
And bars of gold;
Enwrought with silver,
Flecked with gray,

And flossed with wreaths of snow—
The feathered fleeces,
Massive, white,
Float—fair and light,
Along the unfathomed air!
With swinging banners flying low,—
All edged with Tyrian rare,
Where purple sunhues glow,—
Swiftly, smoothly, slow,
Afar they come and go;
Bright Argosies of blissful gains;
The ships and sails that know no place,
The mystic veils of Nature's face;—
Within their deeps, a kindly spirit
Waiting—keeps a watch for Rains,
To bless the patient, trusting plains!

*

The Seasons.

When the long, fair Summer,
And glorious Autumn days
Bide for thy work and shimmering wait
Make haste to think,
To work and say,
By and by,
The rain will fall;
Down over all,
Pour the cold waterfall!

When Winter's discontent
Comes with his murky air,
When leaden clouds obscure the sky,
And raindrops patter down
Throughout the dull, gray day,
Make haste to hope,
To work and say,
By and by,
God's glorious sun will shine!

When the young year says
He cannot stay,
And the bright, quick Spring
 Flies like a bird to May;
Make haste to sieze the passing hour,
To work, and say,
Nor seed, nor deed can shirk,
That would the after Harvest share,
With Rest amid God's bounty fair!

Ay, by and by, the sun will shine,
And by and by the rain will fall;
Make haste to work and say
Meantime, God gives each day,
And Hope—the steady ray,
That cheers our striving onward way!

✻

A Summer Day.

Around the world, the busy world,
The flaming wheel has slowly whirled;
     The Morning sweet—with flying feet,
     But danced a minuet so fleet;
The royal Sun, at burning noon
Soon wilted pleasure—ah, too soon!
     There's scarce a breath to save from Death
     Sweet Life—all panting Nature saith;
Relentless, fierce, unshrinking beams
Upon the dazzling waters gleam;
     The azure sheet—like polished glass,
     Under the glare a molten mass.
But suddenly, softly, swiftly springs
The white-capped breeze on silv'ry wings.
     And gently ripple to the shore
     The undulating swells once more,
While little heaving waves roll o'er
The pebbled strands of Elsinore,

Sweet Life awakes, and Hope regains
　　Her vantage ground of fertile plains;
The pleasant hours revive the flowers,
And work and song renew the dowers
　　Of happy homes; now, whilom roams
　　The hunter—and the white yacht foams
The deep blue water round her bows,
And scuds as fast as sail allows!
　　The quiet Moon draws on apace—
　　And fills the sky; beloved face,
That shines afar—yet always near!
We know she is the same friend dear,
　　To all our loved where e'er they are;
　　The same fair Crescent, guiding star!
Sweet Day has waned—the long, bright Day;
At sultry Noon—we scarce could pray,
　　Till spent was all the fervent heat,
　　Like youth and strength, when angers beat
Their scorching airs upon the soul,
While o'er the heart fierce passions roll!
　　But at the last, Peace is the close—
　　Dear God sends heart and Day repose!

*

Three Fruits.

O, straight gray tree the Savior;
　　O, Olive of Gethsemane!
Grow in all gardens now, beloved,
　　Thy fruit in every land be free!

If men whose strength must be restored,
　　Love racy, fragrant, cooling drink—
They'll try the nectar Hebe used,
　　And make the Lemon aid—I think!

O, Apple of Hesperides,
　　That Paris tossed to lovely woman;
Thou never wast the fruit of discord,
　　O-range!—to comfort every true man!

A Shower.

The blessed Rain! the wilting Earth
Receives and drinks it down;
Raindrops bright glow,
Rainbows Sunlight show,
And everywhere the misty air
Is full of children's mirth!
A wondrous light of golden-green
O'ercasts the freshened scene,
While ev'ry Rose and Lily's cup
Is bent—and waits to be turned up
By the blessed Sun, tomorrow!

*

Degree.

Gray garden Mints,
How dare you grow
Among the regal Roses?
Oh! At their feet, we've watched their tints—
Bright, glowing, crimson, and so sweet—
Till in our hearts we almost think,
We too may grow,
And love as do the roses!

*

The Poet's Wreath.

A garland of gems
Left by the waves of thought,
On the shore of Time:
Woven with chimes;
With mem'ry leaves wrought
With flowers and stem;

Birdsongs and sunbeams,
Greenwood and breeze,
Earthland and star,
God and the seas;
Red roses rare,
White truths most fair,
Entwined with a thorn,
Empearled with a tear;
Forget-me-nots few,
Fadeless, shining in blue,
Like still polar stars
Drawing souls from afar.
A mystic wreath of silent song;
Songs of youth and happiness;
Songs of home and heaven,
Songs of labor, hope and love—
Songs of Nature's leaven!

Book the Fifth.

✳

A STONE OF SARDONYX.

✳

The Choice.

The spirit flies from spray to spray,
From land to sea, from earth to star,
And spans the living, loving heart and hand
Of Nature to find true happiness;
For what doth Nature strive?
For power! In peace and war
Her elements unceasing strive,
And man doth strive—for power!

Why should we strive
Beyond the limits of life's noblest end?
For wealth or fame, if happiness
Be power? And it must be;
For this the world doth strive, it says,
Forever, here and after;
By all means and in all ways,
Thro' time, eternity.

The secret source of power
Is difficulty overcome
By strong determination;
By this all things are won
That can be won,
And happiness may be our own
If we are but determined.
Yea, duty done is heaven won.

What shall one day be worth to me
From out the years to come?
What shall each day be worth, my soul,
To life, to love and home?
Shall it be happiness, true power,
For every creature's daily dower?

Yea, what should power be
But gladness, happiness?
Are yonder stern and lofty mountains
As happy as the humble earth,
That lives and loves with sun
And summer's tender flowers,
With uses sweet and calm content
For man's and Nature's sake.

The mountains, genius, aye shall be
A help and barriers from life's sea
Of storms and windy gusts, but cannot be
The firm foundation of our homes!
Keep near to home, keep near to heaven,
For home is heaven, and heaven is happiness!

What tho' the way is hard,
The morning sun, like Love, is here;
Faithful and soon he comes to help,
And gives himself for sympathy;
And if he is not here, then he will come—
The sun of truth and righteousness;
And we may measure as we like,
Our life, our love, our home and heaven,
If we but choose to win
The dawn of day and Eden!

Then grasp the gift; it is thine own,
If strength and hope and love but come;
Duty and home are one,
Duty is happiness.

Yet love must sing,
The mountains shine
With glory bright and holy,
And lend their rays to lowly ways
And listen to life's story.

The Perfect Day.

Ye hills, ye barren hills that lie
    Forever in my pathway and my sight,
Is there no glimpse of verdure for my weary eye,
    No flowery dells, no trees of restful might?

Beyond the line that bounds my vision, there
    Perhaps bright beauty nestles, waiting long
To show to struggling souls her face so fair,
    Her gentle grace, her truth so strong.

Beyond; forever just beyond the hills,
    That loom so close beside my way,
I'll find my rest, and with reward that fills
    My life unto an endless, perfect day.

A perfect day? What is this day,
    That cheats my weary pilgrimage,
When e'er I reach forth to a way
    That lies beyond the present day?

Oh lovely Future! only near me,
    In the loving, earnest Present:
I shall find thee, only near me,
    When I go to meet thy feet!

What should be done
    Let me take hold and do;
The minutes then will be
    Blossoms and buds for Eternity!

Here is a flower of patient grace,
    It blooms beside the winding way,
And grand and goodly greenwood trees,
    Hard by the rippling stream of faith!

Then on I'll walk, and see thy face,
    Each coming day shall find thee—here;
I have no need of resting place,
    Thou art not far—but near!

A Sigh.

O the past, the glowing past!
 With its youthful hopes and roses!
Would to God they might always last,
 With the life and love Time throws us!

Careless Time! He loves no one,
 He wastes—he brushes the bloom
From the heart and lip—from the brow and cheek;
 He rudely hastes—the bloom he wastes.

Ah, sad the truth and sad the seeming;
 Of Youth's sweet rose we are bereft.
But yet be strorg—for all that's left
 For life and love—is after gleaning.

One harvest is past but another comes;
 Today we may glean the Truth,
With wayside flowers that we may wear,
 E'en down to the end of life,
In everlasting bowers!

*

Growing Old: An Ideal.

Growing older? Growing better;
Casting aside the spirit's fetter;
Seeing a light on a far-off height,
Choosing each day the path of right.

Growing old gracefully? Gliding to power;
Seeing the way with a clearer sight;
Learning to live with a happier dower—
Charity wise, and patience bright.

Who would go back to milk for babes?
Grow old we must—then why not sooner?
There is always younger contrast that fades
And we must e'en pay our debts to Nature!

But have not we a recompense meet,
In flower and fruit from experience' tree?
Charity wise and patience sweet—
Apple blossoms of gold to be!

Bread-fruit from the tree of life,
To feed who need at her door;
Now hath our Adam a better wife—
With garments of light for her poor;

Spinning a precious diamond thread,
She weaves on the warp of time;
While sweetly down her spirit's way,
The bells of memory chime.

Her beauty lives and grows
Upon the food of soul;
'Tis colored by her changing thought—
As the mothfly's cocoon roll.

O Happiness so young and fair!
Thou art Beauty's silent sun;
Transparent—thro' thy shining air—
Perpetual Youth is won!

✳

Resolutions.

O days gone by—can ye return no more?
I hear your voices yet upon the far-off shore;
I know the joyous thrill that lingers with you still,
And melody that Youth can hear, but once for each alone;
That led us on to meet our Life,
In Hope's clear bugle tone,

O happy, golden days, ye golden days of yore,
I stand and wait for you upon a rippling shore;
Ye can return to me upon a silver sea;
The sea of song, where memories throng;

I wait upon the shore
While through the ebbing tide,
The days of fate grow dim,
And drift once more.

Upon the tide, white memories ride ;
They come and seek my side
With faces of delight, with joyous pride,
To be recalled through time and tide.
Sweet, precious friends, where have ye been?
Why went ye not with me?
Did I forget how dear ye were to me—
And waited not when darkness came to ye?

No more—no more ; we'll part no more ;
Together we will stay, and seek the Sun.
Together we will live, till life is rightly won—
You promised love, and victory, and duty surely done.

＊

Work.

There is work to be done,
Ere the set of the sun;
Ere life and the sun
Be forever done:
Then hasten thy feet—
And faint not, O Soul,
The minutes fleet,
Immortal roll :
Not thine if lost,
Too great their cost;
But swift minutes saved
From Time's surging wave,
Make thee, O Mortal,
Put on the immortal;
Such life is a part
Of Eternity;

Oh,—soundeth thy wave
On the shore of God's sea?
Time should be lived;
Then live with Time.
Nor lose Life's race;
Still strive, if thou wouldst gain
A glory for thy pain;
Ere sun be down—
Love's own immortal crown,
And resting place.

*

The Hours.

The pendulum must swing, swing, swing;
Then let the pendulum sing,
Nor tell of the lonely watch
The midnight keeps;
Never the lonely watch,
Nor the hurried fears,
Of the silent years.

The pendulum must swing—
Then let the pendulum sing;
Of a chaplet of hours,
Fresh and fair
As dew-filled flowers;
One by one,
We take up the hours.

Ever, forever, the incoming hours;
Take them up bravely,
Bravely and well;
Take up the rose,
Take up the thorn,
Weave them and wear them—
Christ wore the thorn.
Many the hours,
Many the flowers—
The sweetest have thorns.

A Star.

O soul, to be a fixèd star,
To dwell in power and light,
To be to other souls their need,
Of strength, and love and light;
Within tho' heat and flame consume,
Without the radiance of the star illume!
Souls that are mine,
That life has given me,
Souls that I can reach,
Souls that I can teach,
Such souls have need of me.

Love only is a fixèd star,
No human heart like thine;
On Love keep fixed thy fainting eyes,
Love is a strength sublime;
Love is thy star, thy strength, a sun:
Thy mortal heart, a planet dark,
No innate strength can own,
'Tis Love's pure light,
Not will, or might,
That can a soul enthrone;
'Tis pure Love's light
Lent to their night,
That on bright brows hath shone!

*

O, Sun!

O, beautiful, glorious Sun?
When shall I cease to sing
Thy praise and prayer?
A prayer and tear
I gave to night,
But prayers and praise
I give the light!

Each day I see
Thy face so fair,
So fair and clear,
That has no peer,
Like a bird of the air
I sing!

I sing thy kindliness,
Thy gentle tenderness
That gives to Earth
Such happiness.
O sweet Sun-shine!
O soft Sun-shine!
Like matchless Love divine,
Thy sunrays softly shine;
Thou foldest in a golden glow
Earth's lilies and her kings!

O Sun! Thou dost open some hearts,
Like a fresh, fair flower,
A new blown rose,
And over its field,
Its fragrance flows;
O Sun! Love's sunrays softly shine,
And blossom flowers divine;
Love copies love like thine!

*

Love's Flame.

Ah, Love! come nigh,
With thy blessed ruth,
And chain my heart
To the glory of Truth;
Let Constancy awake
And be my faithful bands,
Fetter my thoughts, my hands,
For the children's sake;

May Patience ever teach,
My ministrations reach—
Surely to them and Thee;
Never an unkind word,
From Self be heard
In deed or thought,—
To those we love—
To them or Thee!
'Tis thus a mother taught
No sacrifice may be in vain,
'Tis thus the World has wrought
The meaning of Love's Name!
Make Home an Eden and children the flowers
That brighten Earth's cares in beautiful bowers;
But dreams of Fame we will not name,
For these are but the after-pain
Of Self's dear song!

*

Remembrances.

Store up Today Love's Sunshine,
For all Life's clouds Tomorrow,
Love's sweet remembrances — within thy heart,
For ev'ry coming sorrow;
And they shall be thy holy balm of Gilead
And shall thy pain assuage
When fear and Death shall come,
And stricken hearts must bleed.

Thy Day.

The Peace of the Hills—
Eternal, serene,
And sunset skies,
Lift up our eyes
To the glory that lies
Round the still and dying Day.

After the battle and storm,
Sweet peace and calm:
The day is far spent—
It's fair life is rent;
To thee was it sent
To give to thy waiting world.

What hast thou done
With its blessèd emprise?
Waiteth for thee—
Well-spent and now free,
A star and a sea
Of Memory and Love, from thy world?

Encircling and shining,
The star and the sea:
Ever thy world
Turned its heart unto thee;
As the Sun to the Day—
Was Love's Truth unto thee?

Shall thy life be received
In a sea of Earthlove,
While shineth thy memory
As a star shines above?

If to a new world
Love's light goeth on,—
Come there ever new souls
To dwell in God's home!

Now and After.

Work thou and wait—watch for God's dawn;
Surely, surely, comes the white morn;
Bright and gleaming, Heaven's golden streak,
Gilds the Earth for the mother meek.

When the red sun all thy days has dyed,
With the spent strength and crimson tide,
Of Life's great work that taught thee Love,
Thy soul wilt have found new Life above.

Perchance when there thou mayst better live,
Mayst better love and truer help give;
Surely the Power that placed us here,
Can answer there the heart's best prayer,
And make this Life as the noonday clear.

Book the Sixth.

✳

A STONE OF SARDIUS.

✳

A Prayer.

Come, sweet Forgiveness, come,
Dwell in my heart like sweet perfume,
And let those odors rise
Of flowers when trampled on;
I need some saving grace,
To keep my soul in place,
To keep my soul in Heaven.

For life is oft a pain;
A blow from those we love;
How shall we win them back again
Without forgiving Love?
Come, sweet Forgiveness, dwell
Within my heart, like brooding dove;
How can we change the Earth to Heaven,
If not by patient Love?

Did not one say,
"Father, forgive them,
They know not what they do;"
So may my heart forever say,
They know not what they do.

*

Love.

Love is a morning glory!
Love is an evening star!
Love is an angel in disguise,
Who found the gates ajar!
Love bears a patient heart,
And hides the wound that grieves—
Love is an angel's sacrifice—
And Love shall be the sheaves!

Love dwelleth on the Earth,
Hath dwelt here from her birth;
She is our hope of Heaven,
Tho' oft by war 'tis riven.
But Joy, bright Joy shall sing,
When Love shall stay her wing:
When garnered all the sheaves,
There shall be naught that grieves.

Love is a sun
For flower and field;
And ferns may grow
In its gentle glow
And humbleness!
Love is a shield
And will not yield,
Patience and tenderness;
But bindeth them fast
To the hopes that are past—
And 'bideth for rest
Within thy breast,
And waiteth long
For his happy home!
Yea—Love did say
For the ancient old,
With heart so strong—
And hand so bold—
"I will be with thee,
Thy troubles to bless;
And sanctify to thee
Thy deepest distress!"

Why.

Yes, yes, I know,
Why cold winds blow,
    Why storms must come
    And hide the sun.

That seeds may grow;
That soils may show
    Their patient tenderness,
    Their willing humbleness,
    Their faithful readiness,
To take the plough-share's steel;
To bear storm throes, then kneel
In thankfulness to feel,
    That Love may come again
    And find a greater gain.

The seeds shall slowly grow,
The spring shall surely know
    Her sister summertime,
    When joybells ring and chime,
When plant and flower haste
Their golden fruit to taste.

The harvest ne'er is lost,
If seeds of Love are tossed,
And Patience pays the cost,
    Till fall the ripened sheaves,
    With falling of the leaves,
    The glory-tinted leaves and sheaves,
That gladly earth and Love receive
Without one sad regret to grieve.

Aftermath.

My soul is swept of fires—
But the greenwood springs again;
After the raging fires,
God's peace and the rain again!

Love's morning dawns once more, my Soul,
Oh, drink renewed thy happiness!
And rouse like springing spears of grass,
Deserve and keep the sweet control!

*

The Heights.

Alone, each struggling soul
    Must bend its silent way,
To yonder noble heights,
    Whereon true Love doth stay.

True Love, that can forgive,
    That loveth Good so dear,
It nobly can forget,
    It nobly doth forbear.

Yea, tho' the way is hard
    And tho' the way is long,
Forbear, forbear, for Love's dear sake;
    Love's gentle, patient, strong.

True Love that pierceth thro'
    The mists that veil the heights,
Transfigures ev'ry hue
    With soft and radiant sight.

In rays of rose and gold,
    Love's morning beameth bright;
And aye we find sweet Joy
    Beneath this wondrous Light!

Love.

Love is a hope;
Love is a pain;
Love is a truth and joy.
Love is a costly gain!

*

Peace.

Sweet is Love's curving mouth,
    Thrilling with restless rest;
Sweet, sweet is the passing peace
    'Neath the deep sea's heaving breast!

*

My Armor.

Good humor be my armor bright,
Encase my Soul in golden Light,
And glint with sheen of shining steel,
That never Anger's sharpened shaft shall feel!

*

Except.

But there is something past;
Forever past; and yet
Life's wine we could not taste,
Except the grapes their bloom had lost!

*

They Cannot.

Oh, there are hearts that cannot feel,
    And souls that cannot fly;
Some souls that cannot, cannot wake,
    So deep in sleep they lie!

Until.

We cannot forgive
Until we forget;
Then let us forget, forget,
Then let us forget and forgive!

✳

Find Thou.

Renew thy steps, refind thy way,
    Retrace, recall the righteous plan;
Along the toiling, faithful way,
    Find thou the noble "can."

.   ✳

For Love.

For Love's dear sake,
    Softly give and softly take,
For Love's dear sake,
    Heart be true and hand still do.

✳

Self Love.

To thy nobler, better self be true,
    And let not Selfishness again renew
The ruin thou must rue,
    The sin that Sin shall do!

A Woman's Heart.

He made me a wife and mother;
　　He answered my young heart's call;
He came, he sought my spirit,
　　He made and fastened love's thrall!

He holds me fast; shall I struggle
　　For aught beyond his breast?
Nay; here is my life's sweet haven—
　　Love hath an indwelling rest.

Back ever my heart must turn;
　　Humbly it sues its own;
Love, "be ye reconciled,"
　　Is the nearest, the dearest, the clearest
Voice of the Throne!

*

Sympathy.

At length I understand
The secret of that sad, deep calm;
She passed him by, her husband,
As one who could not—
Would not—understand
A sympathetic tie!

Perhaps God's angels know,
How helpless—and how lonely—
A woman's soul may be,
Linked to unsympathy;
In them she may confide,
And God alone shall know;
Ah, none *can* know but God,
His angels, and the truth that hides!

Worn.

Over on the other side—
    Unto the bourne so far away—
With eyes of longing look we now,
    We left Life's stronghold at midday.

We left the battle to the strong,
    Amid crushed flowers at their feet;
They know not yet the way so long,
    Their own dear thought they hope to greet.

Renounce your wills—your hurtling strength;
    So shall ye see the Shepherd's paths;
So shall ye hear soft, rustling wings—
    And find the blessed aftermaths.

Adown the hill—adown the slope—
    Across the river to the plain;
There dwell in rest—no more in hope—
    The millions of the worn and slain.

*

Wifehood.

Peace — to thy wounded soul!
No knell shall tell or toll;
Oh, balm and healing swiftly bring,
On some strong Angel's wing!
Close unto his wounded side,
Pressed the Saviour's spear, O bride;
Fast they bound unto his life —
The Saviour's thorn, O, anguished wife;
Bear thy pain as Love, like Him;
Let no tear, no tarnish dim
The brightness of thy wifely crown;
Christ for thee a life laid down,
To show to thee Love's highest crown;
Love's enduring, Love's forgiving,
'Mid Life's striving, yielding, living;
This is Wifehood's highest crown.

Communings.

Each conscious soul must wake to strife,
With its own fate in battling life;
But yet, forget not to compare
One life with many lives of care.

Sorrow is selfish when we grieve
For self and self's dear love alone;
Ten thousand lives are like thine own,
And thousand lives beg Death's reprieve.

Then why not endure all of God's test?
Become thus free; grow strong and rest;
Free from wrong, and th' hindering chain,
Of grief and care and bootless pain?

'Tis written "Seek and ye shall find,"
This is a certain rule and just;
Sooth! Wouldst thou scorn the laws that bind,
And still dost ask for Heaven's free trust?

Yea, thou must conquer self, not sin;
To conquer self is to grow strong;
To conquer sorrow, conquer wrong,
And thus with joy to "enter in."

We need our lot's most hard conditions,
That we may learn Love's sweet petitions;
To make us what from thence may spring,
What good from evils can we bring?

What is the meaning of Life's sorrow?
Ah! Night must come before the morrow:
Sweet sorrow soon has second sight,
And darkness can reveal a light!

Wouldst thou receive naught but the good.
And selfishly reject Christ's food?
Life's good and ill one seed were sown,
Reject the ill — some good has flown.

'Tis not Life's good all tamely given,
That were an easy task to thee;
But ills we conquer lead to heaven,
And crown the soul with victory.

*

Attainment.

Higher, soul, yet higher,
Still higher, wing thy flight;
Live and love
Without sympathy,
Doing the Right!

Tho' thy thought aspire
To all the empyrean,
To the altitude of Truth,
Yet is thy conquered self,
Thy noblest work of ruth.

Tho' the heights be not attained,
Their holy beauty yet remains;
The Right remains;
And Right immutable,
Shall souls sustain,
Till all the mount of God be gained!

All Things.

Stead thee, stead thee, my soul,
  To walk the narrow way;
To climb the holy mount,
  Where God and Love doth stay.

O Love, O Love, come nigh
  And be my steadfast stay,
Come now, dear Love, come now,
  And keep me in thy way.

Love canst thou not be all things,
  All things unto me?
Wisdom, Patience, Faith and Hope,
  Strength and Charity?

Holy, holy, holy Love,
  Faithful righteousness;
Truth, and loving faithfulness,
  God, himself is this!

*

Well Doing.

O to endure—O to fulfill—
  The sweet and pure,
Beloved ideal!
    Not weary nor faint,
But ever intent,
    On each duty bent—
To climb each rugged hill,

Skillful and swift,
     As Angels might lift
Their wings o'er the vales of Heaven;
     Like them would we rise,
Were the strength Duty given—
     For which evil hath striven;
We would mount to the skies.

Oh! God and sweet Heaven,
     On earth be our leaven!
May we fill every breath
     With Christ's spirit of life,
Share His strength in the strife;
     In conquering self
We conquer all death.

For true, the life divine
     Is "not my will, but thine;"
This, O Christ, Thy cross, and mine,
     With its burden rife;
O my brother, friend,
     Blessed Thou—teach me to live,
To the bitter, faithful end.

To lift Life's heavy cross,
     And silent climb the hill;
To do Love's patient work,
     And bear its greatest loss,
If thus it seems God's will;
     Thus didst Thou live and died—
And Truth was glorified,

An Invocation.

O Love, O Love, O Love! thee would I deify;
Unto thy pure and patient soul, serene and strong and high,—
Our poor and weak, yet conscious souls must sigh;
Our inmost souls must reach and faint, and strive and cry.

Unfailing is thy subtle strength, thy true and tender tie,
To show to weary Earth Heaven's sure and sweet reply;
To keep our longing hearts Celestial portals nigh,
And from the "gates of Hell" help fainting souls to fly.

Thine is the Arm of God; He rules when we descry
In thee the power of Christ, to truly live and die;
Thou art the promised vision: our souls and life rely
On Love, the blessed spirit, that God and Christ ally.

Oh heart, look unto Love, and Faith with Love shall vie,
Uphold the fainting Earth, as Love holds Heaven's sky;
Along the eternal valley the olden shadows lie;
But still one star is shining, Oh, Love hath told us why.

Yet Love, Oh, Love, we know thee not;
Fain would our souls comply
With all thy gentle, gracious will, be guided by thine eye;
Amid the storms of passion, the wrecking waves so high,
Love, save us, or we perish; Oh, hear our failing cry!

The Warfare.

Spirit of Love and Life!
    That strivest still with man,—
Oh, rest our souls
In perfect peace—
    While we abide Thy plan!

Possess our souls!
    May we lay down,
As Christ to Thee,
Love's purest crown,
    Humility!

Rest *not* our souls!
    Till patient, we
Agree to all Thy plan;
Until we see
    God—in the perfect man!

Book the Seventh.

✳

A STONE OF CHRYSOLITE.

✳

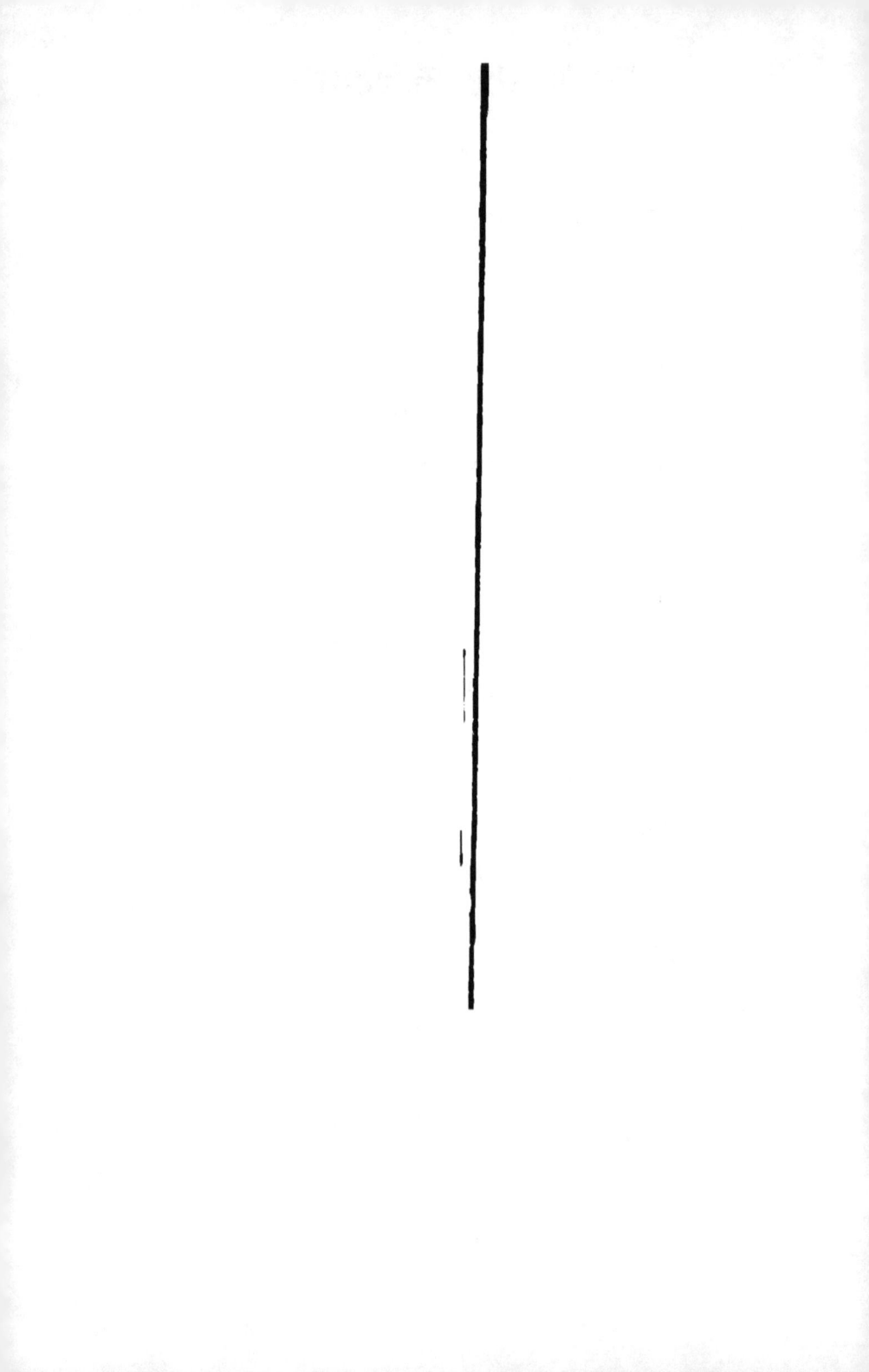

So the Giveth.

That lonely cry,— far off,
In night's deep veil,
What means it to my soul?
An unknown life is there,—
A voice so sad, so wierd, so lone. . . .
Cuckoo! Aha! Is that the cry,
So sudden now, and near?
What now? What seekest thou,
Wild wanderer, in thy flight?
Hast thou no fear? Lov'st thou the night.
The moon and stars are thine,
The sleeping flowers and cooling drops of dew,
The mockbird's nocturne,
And the sea's soft, pulsing beat? . . . .
Thou keepest on a footstool—
Close by Nature's feet!
Thou sendest prayers up to her,
When darkness hides her face,
And ever thus she finds thee,
Still trusting to her grace!

*

The Life of Nature.

O God, Thou art the !oving life of Nature—
Her spirit of beneficence, her infinite, pure soul;
The mother heart of Nature
That shelters all her creatures;
Thou art, indeed, "our Father;"
In Thee and her as soul and body joined,
The wondrous life, the mystery of creation lies.
Thou dost exist: if we have heart;
Then must we see and know the counterpart.

God is the gracious Spirit, power for good,
That shall all evil overcome
As heretofore; th' undying essence
Of Love's aspiring breath,
Blessing each creature and its circumstance.
Yea, have we found Thee, happily know Thee now.
Love hath revealed Thee unto love!
Throughout the universe, beneath
The vast, eternal dome of empyrean walls,
Thro' all the circle boundless,
Pulsates a mighty life,
And orbs of fire, and men with thought, have breath!
Still doth God bring order from chaos,
When moves the pure Spirit on slow, healing wing;
As in the beginning was formed the first thing,
So worketh He wonders while still the stars sing!
Perpetual motion is the rest of Thee—
Impenetrable power and mystery!
Thy living forces, ever undecreased
While stands inertia's law, that cannot cease,
Restrain dark evil's strange, permitted sense,
By sure and steadfast laws, by Truth's omnipotence.
Because God's love with Nature's work doth blend,
All things are overruled to greater ends,
Because God's self is Nature's infinite great life,
The universe of mind and matter is blessedness not strife.
Yea, man may measure many worlds,
But never once — the invisible, the all,
The wondrous, wide unknown,
God's own eternal thought and home!

Both Law and Love.

Tho' burst a sun's bright ball of fire,
New suns are ranged around a sire ;
Tho' planet world turn meteorite,
The aeons bring Love's seeds to light ;
Tho' poison live beside the bread,
God's law of Love forbids it wed ;
Tho' dies a man, his soul's free fire,
May onward speed to his desire :
All things,— Christ's lilies and the sparrow,—
Do know the Love of God ;
What else — a bird's life or a flower's,
But sweet, upspringing Love —
The beauty and the breath
Of wondrous Nature ?
And when the sparrow falls,
Its hungers all are ended ;
God is good ; some gracious law hath understood
Why its short day is ended ;
So, too, both Law and Love may read,
When souls of men are ripened seed !

*

Nature and God.

They say He shows no mercy there
When the Right we did not do ;
Alas ! She shows no mercy here
When the Right we do not do !

Within the Law.

There is a power outside of us,
Outside of Earth; 'tis Nature;
She "sits centered in her myriads" of stars —
And Nature hath done wisely, lovingly,
'Tis only man that mars;
'Tis man in ignorance or self-will,
Who lays the source of every ill.
Ah, Love! God hears not? All in vain,
Our souls cry out in grief and pain?
Ah, nay! within His sure and steadfast laws
Lies hid the germ of every cause;
Nature is Life, she is God's hand and brain,
Hath wrought of self, Life's wondrous, endless chain;
Make haste her loving law to scan,
And lend thy life into the plan;
Then for thine own and others' weal.
Shall knowledge come with grace to heal.

A soul in Nature underlies
Her atoms and her laws; it lives, it flies
Thro' out the Universe, from rock to rose,
From star to sun; and aye, within the Law,
The Great Heart grows; the Omniscient One,
Ascending still, and joined unto her cause,
Inscrutable, still lives *within her laws;*
He dwells in Beauty's starry, sacred soul,
In Aspiration's upward, noble goal,
In humble Duty's patient, labored, strong control;
Transparent germs evolved in light,
Take form and color, wonders bright,
Each one but shares some world's delight;
And to the sphere and sorrowing mortal's soul,
God's times and seasons must unceasing roll,
Till perfect all in Wisdom's fair control;

To outward eye, to inward sight,
He is revealed — the eternal truth, the Light
Divine, in Beauty, Fitness, Right:—
And tho' no form to Spirit we conceive,
Save in the forms that Nature gives—
While Being moves, and Being lives,
Yet in *Love's spirit* may our hearts perceive
The God in whom all worlds believe;
"God is a Spirit," and this subtle sense
Shall still be man's, and ages hence
Dawn into Beauty more intense.
Indissolubly joined, all beauteous Wisdom, perfect Love,
Still must we say, *the Life* is God above,
His spirit and His form — the Universe and Love!

*

Two Kingdoms.

There are two kingdoms — one without,
And one, Christ taught us, lies
Within the heart;
The outward kingdom, Nature's real,
The inner — God's pure, high ideal;
These two combine in one,
Compel us to our fate,
Yet, holds aspiring man the key —
The perfect Good and Beauty of both worlds.

The Ideal or the Real.

The ideal joins the real;
Nature, the real,
God, the pure and high ideal,
The highest height
Of the material real;
God, the infinite, living power,
That dwells within, beside —
Beyond the natural real,
And acting ever, only by and thro'
His own, the embodied real;
The perfect Spirit of the whole,
The Universal whole that shall be all.

Nature and God are one,
Upon the heights;
God is brightest Truth unveiled —
The pure ideal made real.
Christ's Godlike thought,
Is of man's real action wrought,
And its still life or power
Nor measured by its hour;—
The Present is the Future's dower,
And thus with God do we,
With Christ in Love made free —
Dwell in His far Eternity.

*

Christ's Thought.

Help — to the poor and wretched brought;
Salvation — knowledge to the wayward taught;
Meekness of heart — and trust in God, still sought,
While yet we carry on Truth's battles that are fought,
Nor let the good work Love has gained — be nought!

Duty.

O, Duty wears the robe of Beauty,
And sings her noblest song—
She reigns forever in her heart—
She wears her starry crown!

Her soul beams through her eyes
Like light from holy skies;
Like Truth's own ray
Of light and love;

Shining upon her path,
An inward light that burns—
A light unto her feet,
And unto all she meets.

Duty is Love and Duty wins,
By Love all things are won;
Earth has no greater name than this,
For God and Love are one.

Greater than faith or hope,
Greater than Justice true,
Greater than life or death—
Her loving Charity.

And Duty waits;
To enter at the beauteous gate
She is resigned to time,
To time and fate.

She works and waits;
She builds the pearly gates,
The heavenly walls
Of Blessedness.

And holy Duty faileth not,
For lowly Duty
Ceaseth not
To watch and pray.

Patient, earnest, faithful Duty,
Hopeful, helpful, kindly Duty,
With the seamless robe of Beauty,
God-like and eternal,
Is a guide and stay.

*

The Holy City.

To do and be the thing
That is a power for Right,
Makes Joy's pure angels sing,
And hail Love's starry light.

O radiant Love,—thou Star above,—
Thy rays gleam white thro' all our night,
And in the clear and crystal air,
That beameth aye so brightly there,

We may *The Holy City* see,
That shall a rest and refuge be;
There—Truth with loving face and heart,
Bides by all and takes their part.

Truth.

O, quench not the light
Of the Spirit's sweet sight;
   Still not the voice of the soul
   When the floodtides roll.

Truth may go hide
In the light of the sun,
She is so fair and clear;
You may find all the rest
By her light alone,
You cannot find her peer!

Kaleidoscopic Truth,
She turns again;
Within her crystal telescope
Another form and color,
Unto the selfsame star appears!
Turn, turn again, fair Truth,
Unto our waiting eyes!

Truth, that springs on living wings,
Still higher sings and flies!
Her song so sweet, Earth shall repeat,
Till all adown her blessed streets,
With mortal voice yet rythmic beat,
The deep refrain shall swell
Unto a Savior's feet!
Till sounds "The world redeemed,"
Where Earth and Heaven meet!

   Like chiming, clear-toned bell,
   Across a far, far sea,
      Truth calleth, long and well,
      Unto a City free!

Book the Eighth.

✳

A STONE OF BERYL.

✳

Midway: or The Flower of Divinity.

O, the heights and the depths of Infinity¡!
Is it, when questioned, but misery?
    Is the boundless circle from center to span,
    A forbidden realm to the mortal, man?
Do angels guard with flaming sword,
The secret of Life from the spoken word?
    Do they watch our souls from the other side,
    And live with God while our woes betide.

O, winged Thought! Thou wouldst venture far —
Thou wouldst ascend to the highest star,
    Pierce thro' the dark, cleave thro' the gates,
    Enter and know Immortality waits;
Nay, yearning soul, thus Lucifer fell
Down to the awful depths of hell;
    Midway — to the steadfast, Earth is given,
    Thou art God's own — *create it heaven!*

Now is Eternity — God is the Higher;
Endure, abide and carry His fire;
    If thou have strength to bear with Love's grace,
    Thou shalt be worthy to stand in His race;
Yea, could the high heart fulfill ev'ry grace,
Thou shouldst know God, as Enoch His face.
    Love's spirit is God — Yea, Nature, the power,
    That out of her mortal evolveth Love's flower!
Nature alone is the root of Divinity,
But the crown is Love — in Humanity!

*

The Dayspring.

Oh, God, when Thou sendest Thy bright sun and morning,
    Send to my sleeping heart Thy precious shining;
When the wide world is blest with Thy dawning,
Wake my sad soul from its deep troubled pining!

Streams the Light to the green, breathing Earth with
    Love's story—
Unchanging and clear the Dayspring on High;
O Love, lift the cloud-spots that darken His glory
    That ever God's presence may seem to me nigh!

*

The Spirit and the Temple.

The Spirit of Love is naméd God,
Winging up through flame and sod;
    Perfection, Blessing is His name,
    Tho' out of bitterness it came.

Mercy with Justice, still He sends,
Mid all the evils that Life lends;
    And what is Love but all, I ween,
    Of Justice that the world hath seen?

Tho' Judgment fall on striving Pride,
Yet Love may sit His throne beside;
    O gracious Love! thou holy ghost—
    Thou Spirit blest, yet banished most!

Around the Earth, from low to high,
God to each soul is always nigh;
    Ever the just may reach His heaven,
    To Truth and Trust His name is given.

Each in himself must seek for God,
Must raise His temple from the sod;
    How fair the building Christ could raise,
    The world still loves to bless and praise.

Thy soul's the place that God requires;
Amid its ardors and its fires,
    Burn incense and make sacrifice
    To Love, the Holy One;—be wise!

"Like as a Father."

"Like as a Father," the Psalmist says,
That Spirit of Beneficence that crowns our days
With daily bread,
With sunshine and with finer food;
Earth's fathers! Are ye good,
That Christ should reckon you in brotherhood,
And say the bread ye give is good?

Blessed Nature! That could create
Father and child! Her noblest power
Amid "the wreck of matter,
And the crash of worlds!"
Blessed Nature! mighty mother,
That of her virgin Life
Created man — similitude
Of Abba, Father,— that spirit
Of blessing and to bless!
How a father's heart yearns
To bless his child; even so,
Great Nature blesses us,
And lo, with Christ we cry,
Abba, Father!

Man is a child of the Divinity —
The high, the noble, pure,
The beautiful, the good, the true —
That is evolved from the long race of worlds and men.
And tending to the promised Heaven on Earth!
God reigns in Heaven,
Good reigns in every place!
Good is His Holy Name!

God's Kingdom.

"Thy Kingdom come;"
Ah me! my heart,
Hear'st thou the Lowly One?
Except ye be as humble children,
Forgiving, gentle, like a child,
Ye cannot dwell your little space,
Within a Holy Place!

Love led the wise men—
Love was Christ's star;
The guiding star
That led men thro' ages to God!

Book the Ninth.

✳

A STONE OF TOPAZ,

✳

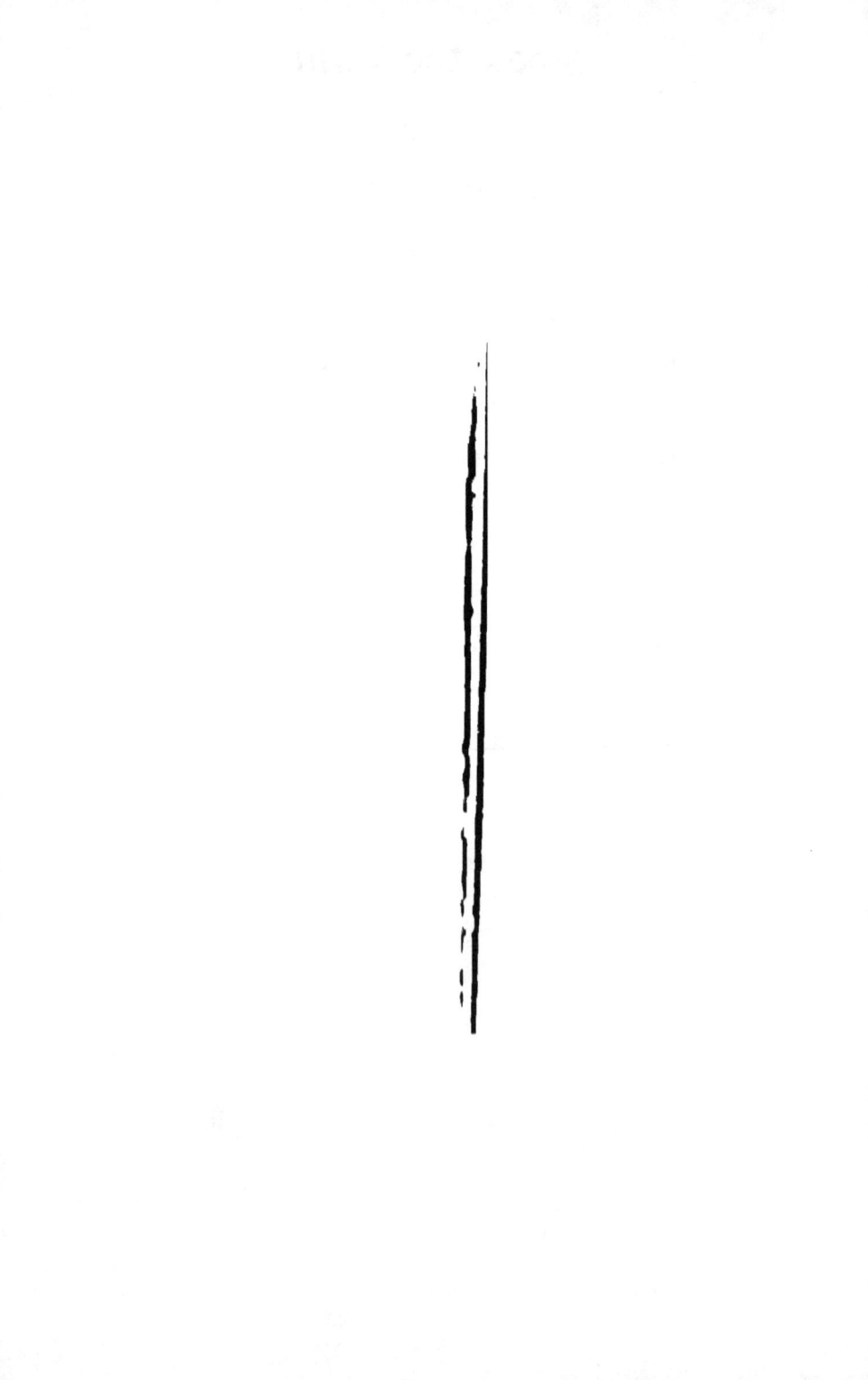

Trials.

I know not how, I know not where,
I only know He answers prayer!
　　When backward I look, far down the dim way,
　　My trials were blessings that I could not stay!

I thank Thee, dear Father, for this heavenly glimpse,
Transfiguring life; my heart shall not wince;
　　Hereafter, when pain may fall to my lot—
　　I'll know 'tis Life's lesson, that pain it is not!

*

Sons of God; or Faith.

Unto Thee, unto Thee be all glory,
　　Unto Thee my spirit shall sing;
Now, as then, with the Psalmist's sweet story—
　　He restoreth my soul while I sing!
He leadeth beside the still waters—
　　For His own name's sake giveth rest;
Ah! God and our Father hath daughters
　　Who love Him as that Virgin blest,
Who took her sweet babes, yea, as from Him,
　　When first to her bosom they pressed;
And tho' man may still cruelly lead them,
　　And the sons from the mother may wrest,
Yet once God gave her his blessing,
　　And close to Christ's life came His power,
Then will He not save to the uttermost,
　　All the world, whom He gave to that hour?

O Lord, help!

Thou canst not find Him
Save in His holy ministers!
Thou canst not look upon His face,
But only join thee to His grace!

Yea, the powers that be
Shall hear thy prayer;
Nay, not that prince, so-called,
Of the powers o' the air,
But those angels God has charged
Concerning thee; their care have we,
Since God, the sovereign one,
Must have his ministers!

O, sovereign power of Love —
Thou Name of God,
The Almighty One;—
How doth thy holy personality
O'ershadow all our helpless prayers!
Yea, if it be "God's will,"
We are — must be — content,
Because his Name—His Name is also Law!
Not e'en His angels live outside of Law,
Then why should we forget
To keep within the righteous way,
To understand the Law?
Some day we'll have God's patience,
And we'll walk in Wisdom's way.

"Our Father."

Yea, bear it all — yet still revere
His Holy Name; "Our Father," God,
Cannot revert the Eternal Law,
But to thy heart He bringeth grace,
He bringeth peace and trust.

That wondrous, all-pervading Soul,
Creator of more forms of Life,
Than culminate in man, the mortal,
Whose power divine is delegated to
The soul, the sense immortal.

God is the Father of thy son — of mine,
If but he call Him by that name,
And blindly groping in his youth,
Turn toward th' unseen Soul afar,
That answers to his reverent wonder.

"Who made us?" says the child; the mother, "God, my son."
The mighty One who made the stars and sun ;—
And does not Science on her rolls of fame,
Say, He is but the first great Cause,
Or Can we find a better, holier Name?

God made us and he leads us,
Inspired souls declare ;
No earthly prayers can change His Law,
And unto Nature, His Interpreter,
Our finite wills must fain submit.

Yea, bear it all, and still revere
His Holiness ; our Father, God,
Cannot revert th' Eternal Law,
But to thy heart He bringeth grace,
He bringeth peace trust.

Jesus of Nazareth.

He taught us to say " Father,"
E'en as the holy men of old ;
He taught us more and better—
To reverence men as gold ;
As temples fit to hold
The witness of God's holy soul ;
As those to be forgiven—
Yea, seventy times seven !
" They know not what they do."

Did He not charge us " work"
While yet it is the Day—
And still, "behold the lilies,"
And trust a Father's care
With cheerful hearts alway?
That Father is the same both yesterday
And to all days, forever :—
So—lives the Master now—with Love and God,
Despite one fearful cry—" Hast Thou forsaken me ?"

To trust in a beneficent Creator—
Do Earth's work ; uplift the weaker,
And keep each man as brother.
" Am I my brother's keeper?"
Yea, what hast thou done
With the feebler one?
Lo, God hath said—the voice
Of that brother crieth
Unto Me, from the ground !

Christ was God's wisest, loving Son,
And Brother to all men;
His meekness was for God, alone
The only Holy One;
His wisdom was for man—do we divine the plan?
"Render to God" true Righteousness;
"Purify ye His Temples,"—ye are His Temples;
This first—then, Cæsar's tithes—expedient,
That Wisdom may be justified.

✳

And Love Shall Be.

I will blot out thy transgressions
Saith the Lord, and remember them
No more against thee—no more:
Neither do I condemn thee,
Saith his Christ;
Go—sin no more—
And Love shall be!

✳

"In As Much."

How easy and how sweet,
The simple draft of kindness meet
When the tired wayfarer's feet
Bring the stranger to Christ's seat!

✳

The Master.

He came before, he culled the olden lore,
Of all Earth's earlier Wisdom he gathered golden store;
He added to it Love; his purer offering then
Was chosen first—of God—and by his fellow men!

Easter Bells.

His star has risen—o'er the world,
And He has risen—in our hearts,
And in the eternal mansions high,
His Spirit hovers—in the Sky!

Nay, till He came—did Love remain?
Did any worship Love? Or pray
To that sweet Spirit ever nigh
To men who as the Dove make sigh

For Holiness to God? Ah, yes,
The Prophets promised men ere then,
The Day should come when all the Earth
Should ring with bells of holy mirth!

When every care should pass away,
The Holy Child become men's stay;
Now with His trust in God, they cry—
We, Father, do not fear to die!

*

Thy Will Be Done.

Jesus of Nazareth resigned
His life, his death, O God, to Thee, ...
This lesson, dear Teacher of women and men,
Thou hast taught it long, teach me!
Ah! The Infinite Nature that placed us here,
That hears our loudest, our silent prayer—
In Youth we turn to the glow of a Throne,
In Sorrow we pray to a Father, our own,
But in Death we know—we are only—God's own!

Book the Tenth.

*

A STONE OF CHRYSOPRASUS.

*

The Soul's Dawn.

Ah! Nature we love, for God is here!
He lives in Law within each sphere;
    Ah! Wouldst thou find his listening ear,
    Then pray to men and God will hear.

Slowly and surely the soul's dawn cometh.
Wait thee, list thee, the day bee hummeth;
    "Behold, I, Alpha, make all things new,"
    And the truths of Omega are also true.

*

The Day of the Soul.

The Star of Truth! O Love, hast thou found—
The "Light that never was on sea or land!"
Lo! It circles the Earth—as God's mighty hand,
With an amethystine, crystal band,
As far and fair as his Science 'round.
'Tis the Star of Heaven! 'Tis the light of a sun
That illumines the soul of the Righteous One!
It fills the Universe, all space and place,
With the clear bright Life of the Holy One!

Truth's star—gleams from afar—like the Milky Way—
Like the Beauty of God with its manyhued ray,
Encircling all spheres with the whiteness of Light
Like that radiant Band that glows in its might,
While His Love is the glory that brightens Earth's night;
Yea, it shines as the Polar Star—alway,
And the star of Life's chart is Love's truth today;
In the Day of the soul, there will be no night,
For men will see Truth as God sees the Right!

Whose Life.

Wherever you go, my son,
Thy mother's thought goes there;
No place can ever lose thee,
From the search of her heartfelt prayer.

Ah! Love—the tides and surges!
Swept back on a mother's soul,
When a man for the sake of a sin will break
The bonds and bars of Truth in twain!

Pity the mothers who shame must bear,
Mixed with their agony of grief and prayer!
Be thou a son—like that Only One—
Whose life set His mother throned on High!

*

The Voyage.

On the voyage of Life each ship is manned,
By a crew of spirits, blessèd or damned;
They toss the bark while the breakers bound,
And lead the soul to that awful sound,
Where Death calls. Come! the port is found!

Sometimes we choose our spirit crew;
If we ask Love's help they are pledged to be true;
But if only we drift—then the evil crowds—
'Mid the wild bursts of passion loud—
Strive in the storms like spray in the shrouds!

Oh, choose of the blessed ones thy crew;
The spirits of Love who wait, and plead
To take us in charge, to bless our deeds;
'Mid wrecking rocks they point, they lead
To Truth—that guides our souls anew!

The Voice of a Star.

One mystic shining Star
Adown the aisles of Heaven,
Thro' all the ages—beams
Its glories from afar!

Along, afar, thro' distance down,
From Darkness unto Light;
It was the brightness then, and now
Upon the far-off heights!

Bright is the nebulous gleaming veil,
Wrapping the dark Earth's toilsome flight!
While forth from the far intangible trail
Springs the white clustering Star of Truth!

Upon the golden sphere
The sunspots must appear;
Before the radiant face
Eclipse and clouds draw near;
But the Sun of Truth shall shine,
The Star of Righteousness is there!

As the Pole Star in night
Is her voice in our flight;
'Tis the voice of our God;
The Angel that bears up the Soul!
O, bright is the night,
With God's ray of Light—
Perfection, the end, and Man's goal!

✳

The Power that Works for Righteousness.

O soul! the good, the power, the Light
Of the indwelling Right—
That can draw other souls and spheres
Away from Darkness' night! . . . .

Does God not say that Knowledge
Is power for good? Yea, Knowledge;
Then more that power the greater good—
And God is only good.
Teach men to pray to Good—
And be a god themselves in doing good,
A gracious god whose name is Love,
And power whose name is Good.
Ah, Love is true God, and Nature the power;—
Then pray to men who love, God hears that hour!
Go seek the Star of Right—
That glimmers through the moral night;
No selfish rights for self—Christ's leaven
Shall help us enter Heaven.
Son, gently yield the way,
And then behold thy sway;
The soft, sweet strivings of the soul
Shall gain Love's place and power!
This world to Nature's son was given—
A Christ to make it Heaven!
Yea, God so loved this world
He gave that blessed One—
To show that men might win
Their titles clear—like Him;
To know thy God is but to keep
Christ's Golden Rule of Rules;
For God is Love and God is Good,
And Love is Heaven and Love is Good!

*

If Only.

Ever beyond is a fair ideal,
Ever beyond—'tis the shadowy real;
And each heart yet its truth shall feel
If only of Life be Love the seal!

Book the Eleventh.

✳

A STONE OF JACINTH.

✳

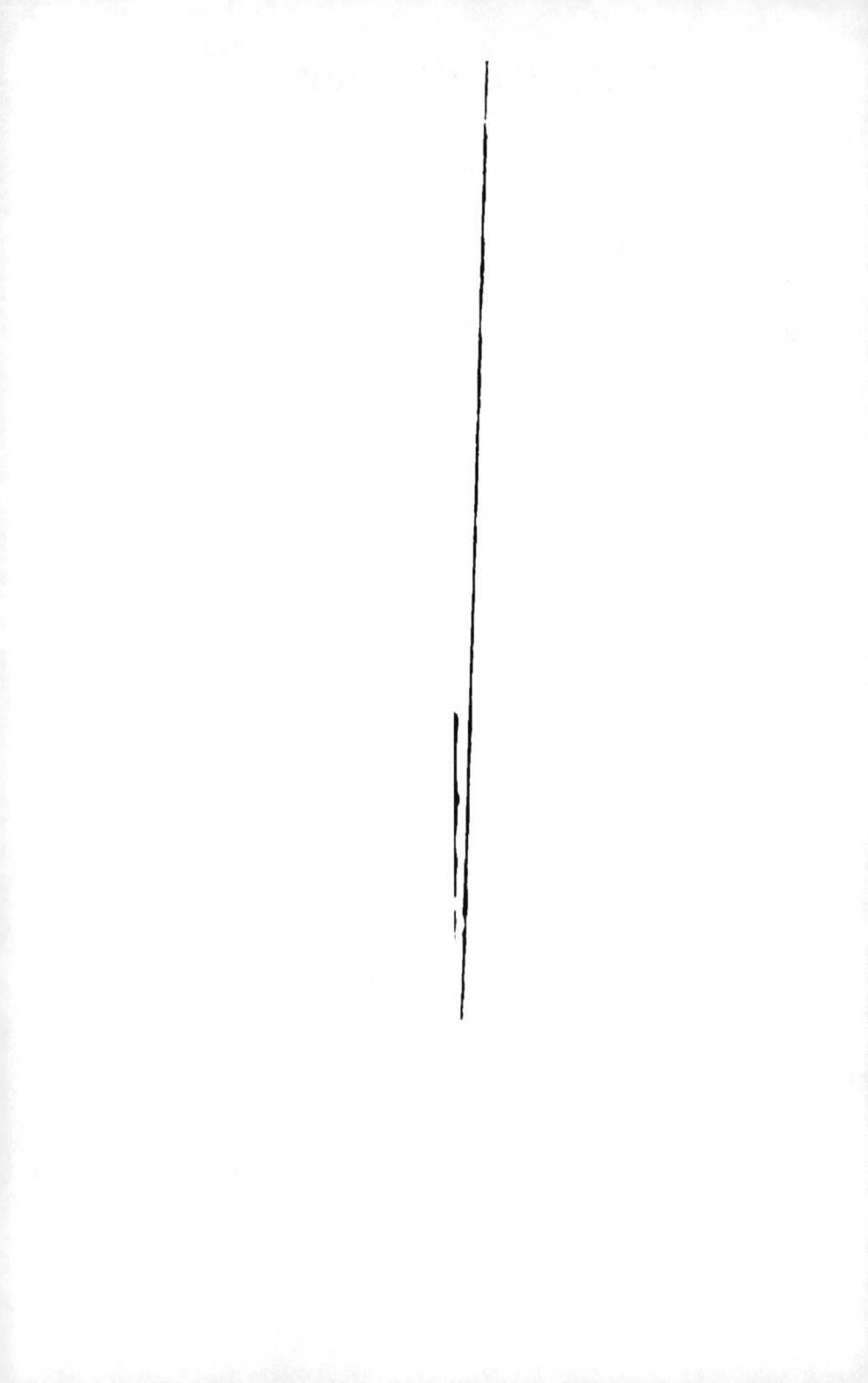

The Spark Divine.

O Love, now shine!
Thou vital spark
Within each breast,
Of God and Truth divine;
Help, spark Divine,
To fan the flame of God,
Within this failing heart of mine,
And mortal truth refine.

Oh, keep alive
Forbearance, Love,
If thou art true;
Does God not promise strength
To every soul that leans on Him
Within its cloistered temple?
Then keep alive
Forbearance, Love,
If God be true.

O, Holy Lord of starry hosts,
Of starry battle plains on high,
Where flash like awful eyes,
Thy comets thro' Thy skies;
Is it in vain glory nigh,
That one so weak should strive to keep
Thy peace — Thy righteousness,
Within a human breast,
And be like Enoch — blest?

Was Christ Thy mystic son?
Once said the Anointed One,
Thy guileless, truthful son,
"E'en as the Father be ye perfect;"

But we—can only worship Thee
In sorrow, while we fail
To be like Jesus, faithful son,
Who could be strong and true—yet dumb—
Before a weak or wayward one.

If God be true,
Love shall be true;
Let wounds and pricks and blows,
Unheeded pass;
There is a life and love
With God, yet not above;
O Love Divine, reveal
In me, the love I see in thee,
And God will set the seal.

O soul, within the inner door,
Lay thou upon the altar,
The sacrifice of Love;
'Tis meet—'tis easier far, and sweet,
This newer gift from thee,
That God requires today;
To prove thy faith in God,
Keep faith with Love,
As Christ hath shown the way.

*

This Grace.

Too much, too oft I strove to carry
      God's cares upon my mortal shoulders;
I now will lay such burdens down,
      They've crushed me oft like mountain boulders;—
The world sped on with mortal fate,
Yet God withheld the awful weight!

I'll trust my dear ones to His grace,
  His Love and righteous Law for them;
And only try to keep my place,
  By holding to His garment's hem,—
That I may find my wandering way,
By Him who is the Light of Day!

A bruis-ed reed He will not break,
  Nor mortal weakness e'er despise;
He bears with all our backward slips,
  As, stumbling still, we reach the skies;
Ah Love, thou art like God—sublime,
With strength and comfort for all Time!

*

Tranquillity.

I cannot sink—He stills the waves;
  I float upon the Living waters;
At last, my ship comes home from sea,
  And finds me with God's daughters!
Within a harbor all serene—
Life's treasure, Love, is brought unseen.

Oh, frail the vessels mortals hold—
  To bear the weight of Heaven's gold;
Of Faith, of Hope, of Charity,
  That Wisdom's holy freight should be;
Yet Love keeps souls upon Life's sea—
Blest with God's great tranquillity.

His Own Abode.

Peace like a river flows over my soul;
    Is it the waves of the Jordan nigh?
    Turmoil and tempest have stranded me high—
But this quiet comes on. . . . . The waters roll—
Away from Life's shore to the other pole,
    And sweep me in—to a haven of rest.

Turmoil and tempest within my breast,—
    The bitter fight with the minions of Sin;—
    But time has vanquished the foes within,
God has given me strength for the test;
Love—for this hour has been my guest,—
    And made my heart Christ's own abode.

Book the Twelfth.

*

A STONE OF AMETHYST.

*

The Living Garment.

Why do the growing trees tend upward,
Why do the happy birds soar there,
Why do the helping winds range upward,
Why does the blessed Light dwell there,
There—in that upper air?

What higher thoughts do the mountains own
To nearer reach the Unseen?
To a greater glimpse of that burning Throne
Whence falls the Light from the Unseen,
From the Soul of God, I ween.

Why do waves of Doubt's ocean lift
Man's soul to its high, wide crest,
But to show Love's light thro' the rifts?
O'er Life's far, deep-heaving track,
God calls the Atheist back!

Back to Himself, the Soul of Nature,
Whose Universe is but our God,
Creating world and Creature;
Her name is Wisdom, Truth and Love,
His wondrous name is—Nature.

*

Groves of Academe.

O God; Thy world, Thine own green world,
Of sunlight and of shade, of latticed leaves,
And whispering winds; of bending boughs,
And little twittering birds at play
Within their downy nests at break of day,
Is wondrous fair and beautiful.
The azure haze of dawn that veils
The sudden glory of thy messenger, the Sun;

The rosy clouds that twine themselves
With streaks of white and golden light,
And glow within the mirror of the silv'ry lake,
Are like the beauty of Thy holy courts in Heaven!
O. what could be more fair upon the upward stair
Than Health and Beauty in this world of Thine!
Man's life is oft a thing too far apart from Thee,
He lives in palaces and hovels of his Art,
Nor seeks the forest and the stream,
Where happier beings dwell
In Nature's true and deep serenity;
Peace, sweet Peace, is Thine,
And sweetly comes to him
Who seeks Thee in Thy Groves of Academe:
Here—In thy templed courts of Earthly power,
Thy creatures all are messengers to man,
And tell the wonders, the goodness and the glories
Of Thy Name!

*

An Unstringed Lyre.

An unstringed Lyre—
Swept o'er and scorched
By passion's fire,
My dear friend's heart!

Great God—great Nature,
What was Thy Law?
What broken harmony—
By her unknown, forgot?

Forgotten Law? Dear Love,
Bring back—bring back
That stringèd instrument
With sweetest sound.

Oh, could her ears
Once more redeem our hearts,
No sweeter song could angels sing,
Nor golden thoughts,
Than we to her would bring!

Ah, friend so dear, thy weakness was
Perchance our fault,
Who bore not greater burdens
For thy harrowed, sorrowing soul.

*

Infinite Law — God's Will.

Thy Spirit—Lord of mighty hosts on Earth,
Of mightier hosts in Heaven, above
This footstool of Thy glorious power,
Is ours to worship when we will:
Thy pure benevolence that planted mother love
Within thy creatures' breasts, Thy message
From the Rose, and clouds of Summer's dawn
From tree, and bee, and bird,
And prophet's Heaven-sent word,
Is ours to ponder long and well;
Thy stars of Night—that hang like glittering swords—
Warding our world upon its sun-lit path,—
Thine oceans filled with wonders to the brim,
Sounding for ages long, their awful spheric hymn,
Thy subtle winds that wander where they list,
That wind and whistle while they rise and fall
In cadences that linger and recall
The whisper of Thy Spirit—bear Thee witness still,—
Yet—mind us of the Law—Thy righteous, wondrous will,

On mount and in the vale Thy thunders sound,—
While the fierce hurricane sweeps round and round,
And lightnings ceaseless play in their appointed way;
Stand off, O man, this ground is holy ground,—
Because of thy poor finite strength, respect, revere thy God,
And learn to know the Infinite Law—His will.

Ah, Nature! Still we love to call thee
By Thy Name of God,
And thank Thee for the old memorials of grace;
To sing: Thou, Lord hast led us on
Thy goodness has prolonged our days!
We know—we feel—while natural law we must fulfill,
No question is—of Love to us, nor Will,
If Death should come, or harm, or grief,
For of Thyself—the Law is made;—in brief—
E'en of Thyself, the Sun, the very airs we breathe;
Nor shall we say that God has bid us grieve,
Because the time is ripe and Law can run
But in the grooves that were before was made our Sun;
Yea, we should know the Law—and if of aught we miss
'Tis not what God hath willed to us,
But of our ignorance this,
Because we recked not of the Infinite Law—His will.

*

A Present Heaven.

Oh, thank the Lord—for ev'ry time
Of beauty and of best!
Another blessed Spring has come,
God's yearly work is well begun,—
The world enjoys the flying moments' Sun,
And e'en the fragrant air—is Love and Rest!

A nearer truth of precious Life
Comes with these glory spells,
And makes us hold our slippling coils,
As firmly as 'twere Heaven itself;
Perhaps it is; this glimpse of growing fields,
That draws us near; these waving boughs of green,
These sprays of pink and white;—
These new bird-songs, this gentle glorious light;
That robin in the path sits listening
As if he heard my every word,
And wondered what comes next!
Ah, Robin, did God give to you
A place within a Heaven, too?
I verily believe He did; for Joy—
He sits, still in that silent mood,
Watching those golden butterflies within the wood,
Those gnats with gossamer wings,
And all the moving, shadowy things
That play athwart the grass and gravel,
And then—he sings! Now and again—
He dances with that small gray wren,
Or tilts a saucy mocking bird!
Robin, Robin, this is Heaven,—
Last Winter's storm and stress were given—
To prove by contrast things are even!

*

Here.

Nature is an impartial mother,
She loves one creature as another,
And in some occult way
She equalizes all within her sway!
Men claim Eternity;

Has God or Nature promised thee
Such Heaven or Hell? Ah, here,
Sometimes it is the one,
And then sometimes, the other;
We live in intermediate states,
And high or low, depends upon our balanced wills,
While God upon us waits!
Yea, God is good; tho' Nature's Law may seem
To lead us down to grief, yet strange,
It leads us up again to things we deem
E'en nobler, better, wiser for the change.
We, selfish—grasp too much,
And lose the willing gift, Today,
Nor thank God for just one
Short, happy hour of Heaven!
Ah, when men conquer Sin
And make of Earth a Heaven!
When men combine in Love
To help, and educate to Love
In all the widening ways
That Righteousness approves,
When ev'ry soul of man can feel—
I love my brother as myself,
Yea, better than myself,—
And find delight in proving
Their hearts are filled with loving,
Ah, then, dear Life's today on Earth shall be
Our certain portion of God's great Eternity!
This much at least has vouchsafed He
To all the meek, and those who seek
Not but to find His face,
His pure and holy dwelling place,
But ever for themselves—some better Heaven!
The Heaven God offers may be Here.
"Yea," saith the Christ, His Messenger,
"The poor, ye have always with you:"

My poor, whose sufferings shall be relieved
By men in Life or God in Death!
Yea, after death is judgment rendered,
By men and God—to all—of all;
By men who dwell on Earth,
By God who dwells in good men's souls,
And in the Ev'rywhere.
Yea, Love hath said—God's poor,
If men neglect them here,
Wake then within some other Sphere,
Where better angels minister!

*

Sparks.

O Lord, Our Father, why are Thy poor—
Unclothed, unwarmed, unfed?
Dost not Thy heart bleed for them?
Are we Thy Hands—
To carry Manna for them
In the world's wilderness?
Thy ravens gather food,
Thy foxes find their furry beds,
And feed their young,—
But the hungry and the naked,
In Thine image made,—
Thou hast left—in cities and by the waysides—
To the growing mercies of his brother, Man;
Ah! the gentle, yearning Heart--
Of the coming, Christ-like man!
Give each of us—O Spirit of All Good,—
Of Thy wise and tender Soul—a part:
Then shall we be vicegerents,
And of kind Divinity—the flaming sparks.

Serenity.

Thou wonderful, beautiful Sphinx,—
    Peace—with the noble, carven face,
    Holding thy quiet thought—thyself, in place,
No matter what the rude world thinks,
    As it jostles by.

*

Every Hour.

Nay—hurry not one day;
Nor wish it gone;
Every hour is a present blessing;
In Earth's uncertain span
We cannot spare one day!

It holds the Light and Youth;
Holds all we know of Hope and Love
Nay,—hurry not—one day,—
Nor wish it gone;—
Love must prize Life's Living Truth!

*

Thy Morning.

Ev'ry morn brings a new day,
A glad new day;
Whether the Sun shines,
Or only Love—
To light the way!

After the longest night,
There always comes a morning;
So—after the night of Death,
It must be then—
There comes another dawning!

How it eases all one's care,
To see the way!
Tho' it may not be—joy,
'Tis blessing that disperses fear,
To see the day!

And so—my Father God, I wait—
Till after Night has passed;
Another Day of Thine is dawning;
If Joy cometh,—
Joy cometh in Thy Morning!

✳

Millenium.

O, since the long years of Earth's fiery youth,
Man has oft conquered by War and by ruth;
But Time softly treads on Love's new-fallen snows,
And gently the old world shall reason its blows!

✳

The Wicked Heart.

What countless ages God hath striven
To purify the wicked heart of Cain!
Witness ye wars and sin-cursed slain,
Ye cruel hatreds that remain!
God is not hidden, nor is Heaven,
And Reason's piercing crown,
On every towering form
Shall change the darkest sin,
And lift Humanity to Him!

✳

The Holy Ghost.

The Father, Son and Holy Dove,
Are Universal Nature, Man and Love;
Yea, we believe the Lord of starry Hosts,

The Spirit and the Soul of Life and Love,
Is maker and the Father of all men;
"The Power that works for Righteousness"
Is one with Christ, the typic Man and Son,
In all that Love hath ever done!
God's breath of Life—in men,
Christ's life—in holy Love,
Combine these all in One;—
The Almighty Father and the typic Son
Show forth one spirit—Truth and Love,
The evanescent Holy Ghost and Dove!

*

Man's Stature.

And if the dead—but cast-off garment be,
Yet still, the spirit of their lives—
Is in the world; if righteous influence, it must be
A blessed breathing Life in mem'ry's sphere,
A holy Light—another's path to clear.

Men are as clay—men are as gods,—
As potter's clay with Nature;—
Yet God has made these lesser gods
With awful powers: with wills that well
Can choose for Heaven, or weakly sink to Hell.

There is no fault in Nature,—Deity;
The sin—if sin there yet must be,
Is in the failure of the creature;
Help—help thy brother, son of man,
To image forth God's nature;—
This is thy stature and His plan!

Speed, speed, O, Heaven, thy coming Day,
When ev'ry man, when ev'ry child,
Shall all be taught Love's way;
Be taught that Love is God,—
If in man's soul Love stay,
Then shall he walk with God!

Praise.

Oh, Life is full of harmonies—
    Of Nature's sweetest harmonies;—
And oft our God hath deigned to bless
    With all Life's power of blessedness!

I thank thee, Soul of Nature's life,
    Spirit of Love, of Hope, of Good;
Of Aspiration's endless strife
    To bring from all things only good!

Hath Nature then no conscious thought,
    With all her various entities?
Yea, Man, with Love, the master thought,
    Doth speak and sing her entity!

Where does the Holy Spirit dwell,
    If not within the soul of creature?
To men with souls the stars will tell
    That God and Love are one with Nature!

Yea, in the depths of man's distress,
    He knows her ministrations;
Her Spirit then is Holiness,
    Thro' trial blessing nations!

Her spokesman wrought! Thus men have fought
    To stand for God; have died for Love and Nature,
Her name have legion angels brought,
    Her messengers are every creature!

God is her power; her power is God's,
    Sustaineth every creature;
Shall I not bless and pray for Love
    To come and speak for Nature?

In Nature is all Life and Love,
    Mind and environment for ev'ry thing;
From man to her shall Love return,
    And with the morning stars still sing!

In Love man finds the entity,
      God's stars for Truth have shone; .
Live for Truth then—Live thou for God—
      Thou'lt live for Love alone!

Nature is the Eternal God;—
      Her perfect human son,
The Incarnate God; soul, be like Him;
      True Life thou shalt have won!

*

The Spirit of Love—A Thanksgiving Prayer.

"God is a spirit; and seeketh such
As worship Him in spirit
And in truth." I thank Thee, Lord,
Lord of the starry Hosts that fill Thy sky,
That now again, Love hath revealed Thee unto Love;
Now as before and evermore—
Thou art the Lord that walks with men
When in the upright heart Love's spirit comes!
All through the human race Thy spirit moves
The hearts of men to deeds of Love, and greater Love;
To swift returning Love that dwells with Thee,
The fount of Wisdom; Spirit of all Life, and source of Truth,
Of all that is in all; well might the Christ of Nazareth say,
"God is a Spirit," and the Prophet say for Thee,
"My spirit shall not always strive with man:"
For we shall know Thee as Thou art, e'er here on Earth;
E'en here on Earth Thy Kingdom cometh more and more,
And wiser hearts shall guide the uplifting hands
That seek to help each brother's mortal needs, and spirit
      needs,—
Who knows Thee not as Father because some error bars
Thy Light, Thy Love.   *   *   * Help, mortal Love,
Thou Holy Spirit in the heart of man,
In ev'ry human life to prove
Thou art the Love that proves the Love and Truth of God

www.ingramcontent.com/pod-product-compliance
Lightning Source LLC
Chambersburg PA
CBHW020014030726
47500CB00002B/586